Didn't See You Coming

by

Gabbi Grey

The Haunting of Pinedale High Series

Didn't See You Coming

The Wild Rose Press, Inc.
PO Box 708
Adams Basin, NY 14410-0708
Visit us at www.thewildrosepress.com

Publishing History
First Edition, 2025
Trade Paperback ISBN 978-1-5092-5942-7
Digital ISBN 978-1-5092-5943-4

The Haunting of Pinedale High Series
Published in the United States of America

Dedication

Axel—for your first beta read, you knocked it out of the park.

Chapter One

Holden

"What do you mean I don't *have style*?" Of course, I used air quotes as I repeated Peyton's statement.

She grinned. "You're out, loud, and proud." She pointed to my button-down white shirt and chinos. "You could do better."

I scrunched my nose. I thought my style was just fine. Peyton was the problem on this front. "Like wear a rainbow flag? Or a pink T-shirt with a unicorn vomiting glitter?"

My best friend vibrated with excitement. "Yes, that's exactly what I mean. New school year—"

"Do you *have* to remind me?" I dipped my fry in ketchup. Lou's Diner made the best fries in all of Pinedale. And the diner was open late, which was a huge bonus. Not that Mom let me out that late—but I liked that the option was there. Pinedale, North Carolina, was a safe town, for which I was grateful. If I *did* go out in the small hours of the night, at least I wasn't likely to be bashed in Pinedale. I could find worse places in NC to grow up.

"You love school." She elongated the O in love to the point of annoyance.

"I don't *love* school." I popped the fry into my mouth. Then realized I couldn't finish my statement without saying more than I wanted her to know.

"If you didn't look like a dork—"

I cut her off by holding up my hand. I swallowed. "Girl, there is nothing wrong with my style."

"It's…like, preppy. Who wears that?"

"Me." I snagged my burger, eyed the size, and decided I didn't want to wind up wearing anything that might fall out. I put the burger back down on the plate and cut it into quarters. "I like dressing smartly. For success."

"Holden, darling, you stock shelves at a grocery store."

I glared. "It's a respectable job. I make more than minimum wage." I'd been there three years and had earned three raises and three bonuses. Mr. O said I was an excellent employee.

"Because no one else wants the job."

"It's a good job." I wasn't going to mention that sometimes he gave me damaged products or produce about to go bad. Those things went a long way to easing the financial strain at home.

"Now, can we talk about *your* wardrobe?" I bit into my burger.

Peyton held up a fry and waved it at me. "No way. You are not changing the subject." She gazed down at her T-shirt, jeans, and shitkicker combat boots.

I swallowed. "Butch lesbian much?"

"Oh, you so did not go there."

"Oh, I so did." I grinned. Neither of us liked labels, so insinuating she might be one thing or another was sure to tick her off. And stop her scrutinizing my wardrobe choices. *Is she right? Am I—gasp—preppy?* "And whose fault is it anyway that I'm out?" This burger truly was the best in town. I focused on the juicy beef patty instead of the echo of the panic I'd felt when that mess went down.

"You're going there again?" She growled. "You always just have to bring that up."

I swallowed and took a sip of my cola. "Look, you were the one who got caught kissing Susan Delgado under the bleachers. Everyone has a cell phone, Pey. You honestly thought no one would see?"

She pursed her lips. "The game ended hours earlier. How was I supposed to know Jason Moskowitz was lurking around with his cell phone? He's—"

"Yeah, he is. And he got in trouble." By then, though, the damage had been done. Kids at school had razzed Pey continuously. Susan's parents had pulled her out of school and sent her to a boarding school near Fayetteville. Personally, I thought that was over-the-top. We felt so bad for her, but Peyton couldn't do anything without making it worse.

Total ridiculous homophobic meltdown on the part of Susan's parents.

"Serious trouble." Peyton sipped her soda. "He's lucky I didn't sue or something."

"Or something." We went over this a couple of times a year.

She grabbed my hand. "But you saved me." She used a heavy Southern accent for that line.

I grinned as usual, hiding the gut-churning anxiety that had led up to my decision. Because between abandoning Pey or facing our classmates out and proud, the decision had been easy. "I came out. Interest in you died down."

Her hazel eyes shimmered. "They decided you were

a better target."

"Helps that you started dating Mark Walker."

"A senior *and* a tight end." She sighed.

I sighed as well. Mark's tight end was epic. And now off at college with a scholarship. I'd miss watching him on the field this year.

He was now on a football scholarship to Baylor.

Peyton had done the kind thing and broken up with him before he left. He hadn't been a great love affair for her, and she wanted him free to date any girl he might meet. Well, at eighteen, they'd be women. I couldn't wait to be twenty—then no one could call me a teenager anymore. Twenty-one would be epic, though. Booze.

"I saw Mark last week." Peyton took another sip of her orange soda.

I raised an eyebrow. "He didn't stay in Texas?"

"He came home to visit his parents. I saw him throwing a ball around with some of the younger kids at a day camp. He's such a great guy."

"Would you date him if he came back?" I'd consumed three quarters of my burger and was eyeing the fourth. I hated to waste food, but I needed to leave room for the chocolate ice cream sundae we were going to share. Without nuts. Peyton hated nuts.

"He's not coming back."

Her certainty caught me off guard.

"That's a definite. He told me…" She gazed around, then turned back to me. "That he's in love with the physical trainer for the team."

"Lucky woman. Anyone who can snag—"

She reached across the table and slapped my shoulder.

I grabbed at my arm and made a show of rubbing it.

She'd barely grazed me. I just loved pretending to be hurt to give her a hard time.

"The trainer's a man." Peyton's glare continued. "That was sexist of you."

"Thinking the physical trainer was a woman? I thought that was quite progressive of me."

"Assuming Mark would be dating a woman."

That had me stopping in my tracks. "So he's…"

"Oh, yeah."

"Did you know?"

"That he was gay? Of course I knew."

"And you didn't tell me?" I arched an eyebrow.

"He was in the closet."

"I'm your best friend."

"And terrible at keeping a secret." She furrowed her brow. "I shouldn't have told you now." She eyed me.

"I can keep a secret." I probably should've been offended. Except she was right—I was a terrible secret keeper. *But outing someone?* That I would *never* do.

"Being outed was tough." She winced. "Having the entire school know I'm bi is pretty…" She gazed up. "Interesting."

"As opposed to the entire school knowing you're gay?" I sat with the discomfort. I loved that I didn't have to hide—being a terrible secret keeper and all—but coming out had been tough.

Especially on my mom. She worked in a factory with a mixture of nice guys and a bunch of assholes. They'd taunted her about me. She hadn't told me, of course.

Kristie Knight had told me her dad was bitching about it at the dinner table one night. He worked with my mom and, thank God, was one of the good guys. He'd stood up for me and my mom. That had irritated the shit out of her because she believed she should be able to stand up for herself. Secretly, I was relieved. I didn't need to worry about her safety on top of everything else I was stressed about. Mr. Knight was six-five and about two hundred and forty pounds of solid muscle.

"Hello?" Peyton waved her hand in front of my face. "You know, we keep having the same conversation. You didn't have to come out." She pushed her burger away.

"Is this because I don't go around with a rainbow painted on my ass?"

She giggled. "That would totally be hilarious. I mean, you would also be naked." She raked her gaze up and down. "At least you're not scrawny."

I raised my arms and did a muscle-man pose. "Must be strong to hold trumpet." I winced as I lowered them. "The trumpet I play badly."

"You should've taken the clarinet like me. Woodwind *always* beats brass."

"Brass is so loud that you can barely hear your little sound."

Peyton grinned. "Oh, brass speaks. I didn't know you could. You usually just bellow."

I pushed my food away. "I won't tell anyone about Mark if you stop teasing me about my *style.*" Then I regretted making the comment, because even teasing about outing someone was shitty.

She narrowed her eyes. "You're not going to tell anyone about Mark because you're a decent guy. I reserve the right to tease you about your style." She snapped her fingers. "Oh, I know."

That rarely portended something good.

"Lily brought home a lovely red sweatshirt. Brand

new, never washed. Very red."

I grasped my pristine white shirt in protection. "You wouldn't."

"Oh, I so would. You'd look good in pink."

I growled. "You're not touching my stuff." I narrowed my eyes.

"Are you finished with your meals?" Morgan stood at our booth, pointing to our plates.

I loved their personality—just sparkly. Today they wore tights and a short skirt under their black apron paired with a pink frilly blouse. The apron was the only uniform in this joint. All the staff were free to wear whatever they chose. Morgan alternated between very femme and very masc. Totally depended on their mood. And if anyone gave them shit, the owner showed them the door and told them to never come back. Given Lou's Diner had the best burgers for twenty miles, she'd only had to kick out a handful of people. Word got around. Everyone left Morgan alone.

"We are, thanks." Peyton waved her hand. "One to-go container."

"Sure." Morgan smiled. "And the sundae, right?"

"Of course." Peyton bit her lower lip. "Because they're the best ever."

Just before Morgan stepped away, the bells rang, and they glanced at the door. As always, at the possibility of seeing someone new, I glanced up.

Morgan whistled. "Speaking of *the best ever*. I have to take care of him, and then I'll bring your sundae." They headed for the door.

My breath caught. A tall, muscular, redheaded god stood in the doorway. With the setting sun behind him, his hair shone like burnished gold. He wore a tight black

T-shirt and jeans that hugged every muscle in his thighs. *Please have a tight ass. I love tight asses.*

"Stop staring." Peyton hissed the words even as the god scanned the room.

He caught my eye.

Our gazes held.

His blue eyes sparkled. Or at least they were blue in my mind. A little hard to see all the way across the diner.

Must just be the light, because no one has eyes that stunning.

The god's attention shifted to Morgan. They were presenting today as more masc but with femme clothes, so I held my breath. The god gave Morgan a huge smile as he followed them to a stool at the lunch counter. *Oh good, likely not a bigot.* That wasn't always a given. Pinedale was making progress—and better than many other small towns—but we still had people who believed I should be damned to hell.

I gave that bullshit exactly the amount of attention it deserved. Namely zero.

"You really have to stop gawking." Peyton casually turned so she could get a better look. Props to her for looking less suspicious. She turned back to me. "Okay, like…I want to say a nine. But rating people based on looks is a horrible thing to do."

"He's an eleven anyway." She was right about judging someone by their appearance. That being said, I knew—on a good day—I was about a seven. Medium height, slender build, medium-brown hair and medium-brown eyes. I wasn't a troll, but I just didn't stand out from a crowd.

The god did.

Morgan was tall, but the redhead was half a foot

taller. Easily. Maybe even more.

"One ice cream sundae with extra chocolate. And two spoons."

I nearly leapt out of my seat as I'd been distracted by the god and hadn't seen Morgan coming.

They placed the food as well as my to-go container on the table. They smiled. "You can pay at the front."

"Did you get his name?" I leaned toward Morgan. They were always a font of information.

They rolled their eyes. "Oliver, and he's new in town. Starts school tomorrow. I don't know where he's from or why he's here."

I took *here* to mean the diner. Although maybe Morgan meant Pinedale.

"Well, we don't have time to sit around and wait for you to interrogate him." Peyton arched her eyebrow at me, then checked her phone. "Your mom leaves for work in thirty minutes."

Wincing, I nodded to Morgan. "Thanks." I leaned over. "But later, right?"

They grinned. "There is such a thing as server/customer privilege."

"Ah." If anyone was a bigger gossip than me, it would be Morgan. "See you tomorrow?"

"Yeah." They wrinkled their nose. "I hate school."

I almost asked if they'd gotten any more modeling gigs in Raleigh. If they hadn't, though, it might make them sad for me to bring it up. "Thanks."

They smiled, pressed a hand to my biceps, and said, "Yeah, anytime." Then they were gone. They'd once asked permission to touch us. As I suspected they didn't have a lot of affection in their life, Peyton and I readily agreed.

I watched them sashay over to the new guy. "Oh man, Peyton. That's the type of boyfriend I want. He reminds me of that hot Scottish guy my mom's in love with."

"Hot Scottish guy? There's a Scottish guy in Pinedale?"

My gaze snapped to hers. "What? No." I waved her off. "Some television show she loves to watch. I dunno…I think based on a book. He's hot. So's the villain, though. Hard to pick a side."

"You always pick the side of good."

I cocked my head. Did she mean people should always pick the side of good in general or that I usually picked the side of good? Pretty much, though, she was right either way.

"He is hot." She fanned her face as I dug into the sundae—ensuring I got my fair share of chocolate gooey goodness.

"How hot?" I squinted. This time at Peyton, not New Guy.

She grinned. "I don't think I'll go after him. I mean, he's super cute, but not really my type."

I blinked. "Peyton, sweetie, you don't have a type." I considered. "And I thought you had a crush on Juliette?"

"Yeah, well, Juliette's one hundred percent straight." She held out her hand and enumerated. "She's so pretty. She goes out with Lucas, the football captain—who also happens to be the quarterback. She's, like, one of the smartest girls in school. And finally, she's the most genuine." She raised her last finger. "My life sucks. I hate that I'm in the band in this dorky uniform while the beautiful, lovely Juliette is captain of the cheerleading team."

"Yeah, that really sucks."

Across the room, Oliver grinned as Morgan handed him…a basket of breaded shrimp.

Ew. Fish. Still, I could learn to love shellfish if it got me closer to the hottie.

"Holden."

My attention snapped back to my best friend. "What?"

"We were talking about my love life. Or the lack thereof." She frowned. "And anyway, loser, you're not even paying attention to me. What would you know about being in love? You claim you're gay, but you don't date."

I narrowed my eyes. "Screw you. Who the hell am I meant to date? Rodney Fulham? Yeah right. The guy is an asshole. He gives all us queers a bad name. And by the way, the school isn't really overrun with gay teens out of the closet."

"Yeah—it sucks. I keep hoping for more of us to come out."

"Besides Rodney."

She made a gagging sound.

Since she'd consumed a good portion of our sundae, I dug in and—

"Oh God."

Belatedly, the sound of the bells registered. Peyton had turned much quicker, but now she turned back, her cheeks flaming red.

Somehow, when I glanced over her shoulder, I wasn't surprised to see Juliette Carver sashay into the diner and up to the counter.

Peyton snuck another glance, then returned her gaze

to mine. She leaned in. "I love when she wears her hair natural like that. Those curls are to die for."

"She pulls it back into a ponytail for cheerleading, right?"

"Yeah. I like the kinky curls."

"Kinky?"

She swatted my arm.

I laughed. Then I could admit the curls were stunning and memorable. Much like the young woman. The object of Peyton's forever crush. Her skin was flawless, her figure was to die for, and she was just about the nicest person in the school. She stood in stark contrast to the newcomer, with her skin so much darker. "You know, they would make a cute couple." I subtly indicated Juliette and New Guy.

Peyton glared. "You stick to your guy, and I'll stick to Juliette."

"What about Lucas, the quarterback?"

She winced. "Yeah, you're right. I know you're right."

"Well, assuming my redheaded dreamboat starts at Pinedale High tomorrow, we can both gaze from afar."

"You're not going to talk to him?" She tilted her head. "You could easily be the welcoming committee."

"And he's probably straight."

"As you pointed out, you don't wear a rainbow on your bum. You could befriend him, and then if he turns out to be a homophobe, you can always walk away. Although—" She snuck another peek. "—judging by all the smiles he's giving Morgan, I just don't see it." She shoveled all my leftover food—as well as a few french fries she hadn't eaten—into my container. We didn't talk about the fact I shouldn't be spending money on going out. This was my one treat for the week after all the hard work I did.

I'd also taken on a ton of extra shifts over the summer when everyone else in the store took their vacation. In the end, I'd had a few weekends free but had worked just about every day since. I gave some money to Mom—which she hated and still accepted—while putting the rest away in a college fund for myself. A bit of a dream, but maybe with a scholarship… And if I didn't get in, then I'd just work extra hard to make certain my younger sister, Isabella, got to go. Damn kid was so damn smart. As she was twelve years old, we could leave her alone, and we did sometimes, but if I could be home when Mom wasn't, I did it. At least with Mom working the night shift, she was around the house before and after school—sleeping while we attended classes. "We need to go."

"Yeah." Peyton pushed out from the booth and pasted on a smile.

Juliette now sat next to New Guy, and they were chatting with big smiles as his food obviously grew cold. *Yeah, she's just that friendly. That awesome.* And I honestly wished Peyton could find a queer girl like her. That didn't seem likely these days. *Not happening.*

Just like you can drool over New Guy, but you can't have him. I understood statistics. More people were straight than on the rainbow spectrum. *Oh well, at least I can watch him from afar.*

Peyton and I paid for our food, thanked Morgan, and headed outside.

I held the door for Hank, our school custodian, as he made his way in.

He offered what appeared to be a genuine smile of

thanks and nodded.

I nodded back, then snagged Peyton's arm.

The bugs got busy on us as we walked back to our houses—which were just a block apart. We'd met while in kindergarten and had been inseparable ever since. While Peyton was happy in our sleepy North Carolina town, I wanted out. To see the world. At the very least, to get a car. With how close we lived to school, I couldn't justify a car now, even a beater, but I really wanted to see something more than these boring six-square miles.

"You going to be okay tomorrow?" Peyton cocked her head.

"Why wouldn't I be? It's just senior year. I'm already out. The hard part's done. What could possibly go wrong?"

Oh, if only I'd known.

Chapter Two

Holden

"Why are we hanging around outside?" I squinted in the bright sunshine. "Really, Pey, what's wrong with inside? You know, where the classrooms are?"

The good news was we were assigned the same homeroom. The bad news was I had old Mrs. Bletchley for algebra while Pey had super-hot Mr. Haley. I didn't use the term *old* lightly. Mrs. Bletchley had taught Principal Kouriki, who'd been a student…I wanted to say in the eighties, but my ability to figure out ages and decades was always lacking.

Anyway, Mrs. Bletchley should've retired a million years ago. But her husband had died in a bombing in Beirut, like, forty years ago. My mom had explained it to me one day when I was bitching about the…older teacher. Mom had said I needed to show respect. The bombing had been even before she was born, but her mother had shared the story and how the town pitched in to support veterans' families, since Mom had whined about Mrs. Bletchley as well. I missed my nana. She would've been about Mrs. Bletchley's age if she hadn't died in her sleep of an aneurysm about ten years ago.

Shaking myself out of my thoughts, I nudged Peyton. "You going to answer me? I'm going to get sunstroke."

"Because you have a lily-white ass."

"You might keep your brains in your ass, but I don't. Anyhow, I worked in the grocery store all summer. Unlike you, who were out in the sun." I was slightly envious of Peyton's glow. She wore sunscreen religiously, but she still had a bit of color from her time as counselor at the Owls' Summer Camp. I'd been thrilled Isabella attended several weeks—that gave Mom and me less stress when we knew where she was. When she arrived home, she had so many projects to show us. So much knowledge to share. I loved her enthusiasm. Was glad that she hadn't necessarily seen the tougher side of life. I might only be five years older, but I'd lived a whole lot more.

Peyton extended her arms. "At least my tan's even this year."

I flashed back to the year she'd gotten a sunburn on one side of her face but not the other near the end of the summer. She'd returned from camp with uneven coloring and no logical explanation. I figured it had something to do with Lana O'Donnell being a counselor that year and the huge crush Peyton'd had on the girl.

I never asked and Peyton never told.

"Oh, there's the new guy."

Following her gaze, I caught sight of my copper-haired hottie sliding out of a nice electric SUV. Top of the line. I squinted again and saw a Black man in the front seat, waving at the hottie. My mind flew over any number of possibilities from stepfather to father of a friend to some other relation. Likely not father, because of their coloring, but genetics was never my strong suit. Regardless, the man's suit was snazzy and smart. Like the kind of suit I planned to wear when I got a proper job.

Hottie paused, said something to the man, gave a brief salute, stepped back from the SUV, and shut the door. He watched as the man drove away. Again, he wore a tight black T-shirt with some kind of logo I couldn't see from this far, and jeans that fit oh so snugly.

Please turn away from me. I want to see your ass so badly.

He turned away and was swinging his backpack over his shoulder when a group of guys approached him. I counted at least six or seven. Football, basketball, and lacrosse seemed to be represented. All jocks. I focused as best I could. Oh, good, at least three homophobes in the pack.

Dominic grinned. "You're new here."

In response New Guy smiled back. "Yeah."

Gary gave him the once-over. "You play?"

"Yeah."

Larry, the tallest of the bunch, asked, "Which game?" Probably sizing up to see if the new guy might play basketball.

"Uh, football."

Dominic smacked him on the arm. "That's great news. And that was a cool car. But you couldn't find a White chauffeur?" He guffawed.

So did the other two.

The new guy blinked several times, then cleared his throat. "He's…he's my uncle."

"If your mama says so." Gary snickered. He played lacrosse and didn't always have time for football players. Well, except Dominic. *Birds of a feather…*

Even from this distance, I couldn't miss all the color draining from Hottie's face.

Peyton dropped her backpack and headed their way.

I couldn't hear what the guys were saying now, but I'd always accused Peyton of having superhero hearing. All the while being totally jealous. In solidarity, I laid my backpack down gently—didn't want to squish my ham sandwich—and headed after her. I caught some of the taunts in a disjointed sort of way, and my stomach churned. Fucking assholes. Here, I'd thought they'd save the racist shit for the Black kids. Apparently, I was wrong.

Hottie said something about his aunt being his mother's sister. None of this mattered. He didn't owe anyone an explanation.

That just made the taunting worse.

I tried to snag Peyton before she shoved her way into the crowd, but like most things having to do with her, I didn't stand a chance.

She stuck her finger in Larry Arnold's face. "You play basketball with Black kids. How can you say shit like this?" She whirled on Dominic Maxwell. "Your sister married a wonderful Black man."

Dominic visibly bristled. "I'm not responsible for what my stupid sister does."

She put her hands on her hips. "You want me to tell Janice what you're saying about Black people?"

"What the fuck do I care? Be a snitch. Figures, coming from someone like you."

"Harrumph."

I totally wouldn't put it past Peyton to text Janice, her older sister Lily's best friend, and tell the woman everything.

"Beat it, pipsqueak. You think you can threaten Dom?" Gary tried to knock Peyton out of the way.

I pushed into the group as other kids surged forward.

"Fight! Fight! Fight!"

Oh, for fuck's sake. "Peyton?" I tapped her shoulder. "Could we talk?" I might've used my sweetest possible voice. Not too high, because I didn't need to remind this testosterone-driven crowd that I was gay. Not all racists were homophobes—but I'd discovered some definite crossover.

"I've got this." She glared at Larry. "You really want to start something? Because I could tell everyone that—"

"What is going on?" Principal Kouriki's voice carried right through the group.

Gary and Dominic took steps back.

Larry growled. "You better not, bitch."

"Mr. Maxwell." Principal Kouriki wasn't loud, but she sure had menace down to a science. She was petite at barely five feet, but she packed a wallop of unspoken power conferred upon her by her title. Her voice carried across the lawn.

But I wanted to know what Peyton was going to say. Not if her speaking whatever truth she held got her into more hot water…but a guy had curiosity needs to be met. And I wanted to know Larry's secret. Because that douchebag was a racist and a homophobe. I'd learned to avoid him in ninth-grade gym class—and I hadn't even been out back then. *Good instincts*.

"I didn't say anything." Larry put on what I could only describe as the most pathetically insincere innocent face I'd ever seen.

I doubted Principal Kouriki was fooled…but she appeared willing to let it go.

She glared. "I'm certain I didn't hear racist taunts. I'm certain I didn't hear threats. And I'm most certain I didn't hear chants of *fight*."

"No, ma'am." Most of the boys who'd circled Hottie said the words. After a beat, Larry added his acknowledgment.

"Class starts in ten minutes." She started to turn when she appeared to notice Hottie. "Are you Oliver Barton?"

Hottie's cheeks turned a fetching shade of crimson. "Uh…yes, ma'am. Oliver Barton."

I blinked. Okay, absolutely not southern. I didn't know from accents, but I knew this kid was definitely not from around here. Not from anywhere in Dixie, as far as I could tell. *You got that from five words? Sheesh.* Still, *ma'am* had a distinctive sound to it when any of us said it.

"Well, come with me, young man. Coach Pinker has been waiting for you. The best kicker in the Pacific Northwest is going to make a fine addition to our team."

Oh God, his ears just turned red.

"Well…"

"Fifty-nine yards." Principal Kouriki gave him a broad smile.

Several of the guys gaped.

I honestly didn't pay enough attention to football—what with having my trumpet to occupy my time. If the slackened jaws were any indication, this was a big deal.

I pivoted to Oliver. Quietly, I whispered, "You met the biggest school assholes on day one. Are you okay?"

He cleared his throat, meeting my gaze with those stunning ice-blue eyes. "I have to go but, uh, thanks."

As Principal Kouriki beckoned him toward the school, several of the boys started to crowd Peyton.

I snagged her arm and dragged her through an

opening. As the bell rang, I hissed, "Stay away from them. You're going to get us all killed."

She snickered.

I was about to call her out on her shit when I spotted Juliette watching us. Since I considered her a friend, I waved behind Peyton's back. Since I didn't need grief in my life at that moment, I didn't point her out to Peyton as we entered the school. We made it to Ms. Cracken's homeroom class just in time for attendance. Since she also taught AP English, Peyton and I would be sticking around for first period with her.

Holy crap, that was way too close for comfort.

That thought carried me through to second period when I wound up in the library, checking out the various novels Ms. C put on our syllabus. We were required to read two, and to my joy, she'd included several books that had been banned in other jurisdictions. I might take a trip into Raleigh with Peyton to visit one of the LGBTQ-friendly bookstores, but if I could find a book here, that was definitely cheaper. We could borrow Peyton's mom's car, but we still had to pay for gas. Plus whatever I'd spend on the book itself.

Oh, cool. I snagged a copy of a book written by a queer author I admired. I'd seen him on television a couple of times, and he'd been on some podcasts as well. His book was on the approved list, and to my delight, the book addressed racial issues as well. This made my little progressive heart sing. And had me making plans to keep it hidden in my backpack until I got home. No point giving the bullies something to razz me about. *Fuck my life.* I sighed, thinking about Oliver and how I wished I knew how he felt about gays. His confusion at the racism seemed odd to me, but then he wasn't from around here, so maybe that explained it.

"That's a big sigh."

I glanced up, then pivoted my head both left and right.

No one.

"Uh, where are you?"

"On the other side of the stacks."

"Okay…"

"What was the sigh for?"

I glanced around but didn't spot the librarian. "I was thinking *fuck my life* or some variation of that."

The guy giggled. "I love that expression."

Okay, slightly weird thing to say.

"Why is your life messed up?"

"Well, I might be the stupidest idiot in the idiot pool." Mom said not to use that word, but it totally fit my situation. Plus, I wasn't calling someone else that name. Nope, this was aimed directly at myself.

That made the kid chuckle. "Okay…why?"

I sighed again. No one was around, and I couldn't see the kid, and he couldn't see me…was this what confession was like? *Forgive me, Father, for I have sinned?*

"What exactly did you do? Today's just the first day. Heck, we're only in second period."

I ran my fingers along the spines of several memoirs. "Did you see the new guy out front? The one Principal Kouriki said was some kind of football hero, the one with the Black uncle?"

The kid chuckled. "I might've. Through a window, of course. He was one fine specimen, for sure."

Huh. Okay. So was this kid one of the closeted ones in the school? Or just super friendly? "You thought he was gorgeous?"

"Of course. I mean, objectively, he's stunning. With the red hair? Yeah, he's cute."

I could hear the smile in his voice. "I just…noticed him." *Forgive me, Father, for I have sinned.* I was about to spill my guts to a stranger, and I wasn't even that concerned.

"And," the voice prompted.

"Well…" I shrugged, even though my erstwhile companion couldn't see. "I don't know much about him. So this is a crush, right? Based on physical attraction. And I swore I'd never do that—"

The kid sniggered.

"What?"

"You're a teenager. That's pretty much the definition of every teenager I've ever met." He paused. "Well, and many adults, although I've met fewer of those. Few and far between around here."

"I should hope so. Unless they're teachers." I shook my head. "Have you ever had a crush on someone unattainable? A person so perfect that they're clearly way out of your league?" I imagined my hands roaming over Oliver's perfect body. The body of a football player, no less. *How is this my life? I'm going to see him all the time.*

My companion responded after a long pause. "Well, yes, I have."

"Okay." I gnawed my lower lip. "How'd that work out for you?"

"Not so good." He laughed derisively. "Why do you think I'm hiding out in the library?"

That hadn't occurred to me. I'd assumed he was just perusing the shelves like me. "So what are we going to do?"

"Uh, I don't know. You got any ideas?"

To help you? Hell, I can barely help myself. "I'm thinking of moving states…" That might've been a bit of an exaggeration. But not much. Peyton had stood up to a pile of bullies this morning. I'd tried to get her to stop and to come away with me. My best friend had a tendency to run her mouth off. Not everyone around here was accepting—although most were.

Then I thought of my mom and Isabella, and I knew I wasn't going anywhere.

The kid huffed. "Come on—it can't be that bad."

"Uh, yeah, it totally can. I'm gay. I have a crush on a straight guy. It's goddamn humiliating and painful. No one understands." Well, Peyton sort of did. Because of how she felt with Juliette. But being bi, she had so many choices while I was limited to five percent of the school population, most of whom were invisibly closeted.

"I do."

I'd lost my train of thought. "What?"

He sighed so loud even I could hear over the stacks. "I'm…gay. I've never said that to anyone before."

I waited for more, but nothing came. "You mean, you're not out?" *Well, duh. I know just about every kid who's out…and there aren't many. Chances are I'd know him.*

"Heck no!" His shock couldn't have been clearer.

"Okay." I paused. "Why not?"

"My dad would kill me."

That sucked. Something I couldn't relate to. When I'd come out, Mom hugged me and said she'd always suspected but was super proud I'd found the courage. I'd told her two years before bursting out of the closet to support Peyton in her little clusterfuck of a disaster after the Susan-kissing incident. "Your parents aren't accepting?"

"Heck no!"

His vehemence caught me off guard. "Well, that's sad. And by the way, you're kind of weird. Why do you say *heck* all the time? Is your family religious? Why don't you just say hell?" I might've glanced around to make certain we were alone before letting another one rip. I used swear words liberally—just not in front of any adult. With the library being renovated because of last year's fire, I still didn't know the acoustics.

I especially didn't want to swear in front of my mother. She wanted me to be a *good, respectful* boy. I snorted. If only she knew.

"Well, uh, we don't swear nearly as much where I come from."

Okay, I just had to see if I recognized the guy. I didn't know *everyone* at the school—but just about. I scooted around the stacks and stopped short, finding the object of my curiosity sitting on the floor. "What the actual fuck? You're naked?" I was trying not to be judgmental, but I didn't understand. Flashers generally wore a coat over top, and they, like, *flashed* their erections. If I ever saw a guy do that, I planned to laugh. Except if he was cute. Then I might—

Oh my God, you are so *getting off track.*

This guy was cute. On the scrawny size, but with sunshine-blond hair and deep-blue eyes. Not the same shade as Oliver's…but they made me think of my crush. Which almost knocked me out of my apathy. Seeing a naked kid in the library did the rest of the shove out of complacency and into the need for action. "Why are you naked?"

"Not by choice, hence I'm hanging out in the library and not in the hallways."

I blinked, noting in the back of my mind that he hadn't actually answered my question. I tried a different tack. "Do you want me to, I don't know, get you a shirt or pants from somewhere? I've got a spare shirt in my locker in case I spill on myself." Which happened way more than I would've liked—which meant always having a spare shirt. The guy was scrawnier than me— and he appeared to be shorter—but my shirt would at least cover some of that very bright white skin. And on him would drape low enough to hide the naked dick I was carefully not looking at. *Not.* I dragged my eyes upward. "Or, like, pants from one of the kids in gym class?" Which meant actually going to the gym…but I was nothing if not helpful.

"Nah. It's cool. You'd better go—bell's about to ring. I'll sneak out later." He rose, giving me an interesting view of his dangly bits.

Although I liked to think I didn't have a *type*, I felt zero attraction to him. "Well, okay." I waved, rounded the corner on the stacks, grabbed the book I'd nearly abandoned, and headed toward the exit. A weird whistling sound caught my attention.

When I glanced back to where the kid had been, I saw no one. There was nowhere for him to have gone, but the space between the stacks was empty. *Weird.*

I returned to where his bare feet should have dented the plush new carpet and peered between the books on either side, looked up at the top of the shelves, even tapped the floor for hollow sounds. Nothing. Nada. The guy had basically vanished.

In desperation, I sniffed the air, wondering if I could smell sweat or cologne. All I smelled was dusty books and fresh paint.

He must've hurried off. Maybe there was a door…somewhere.

Maybe I'm just seeing things. Like how I thought I saw something in Oliver's eyes for the few seconds we locked gazes. Which was as delusional as seeing a naked kid in the library.

Am I going nuts? I gave a hollow laugh. "Yeah, you dork, so hard up for a date you're imagining naked dudes." Surely, the blond guy was there. I didn't imagine someone coming out to me. He just left. To get some clothes. Obviously. I'd see him around school sometime, and we'd laugh about the library naked confessional, and I'd find out his name. Logical. Reasonable. After I gave my head a good shake, I checked out the book and headed for lunch.

Chapter Three

Peyton

"You manage to get your trumpet out of your ass yet?" I glanced over at my so-called best friend as he polished his instrument. So-called because Holden pulled me away from that fight this morning before things had gotten interesting. I hadn't finished giving Larry, Dominic, and Gary a piece of my mind. Jesus Christ. Assholes.

In my head, I gave the sign of the cross for taking the Lord's name in vain. My grandmother would be rolling over in her grave.

"My trumpet doesn't fit in my ass." Holden turned his glare on me. Those brown eyes said so much. Part amusement, part tumult.

"Well, my clarinet would." I held it out with pride as I'd just replaced the reed.

He arched an eyebrow and gave me his patented *do I look like I was born yesterday* glare.

I giggled.

Clapping from across the field drew my attention. Ah, the cheerleading squad practicing some of their trickier maneuvers. I was super glad Juliette wasn't a high flyer, because my nerves couldn't have withstood that. *Right, like you have any claim on her anyway.* She was in the front row, doing a backflip, ponytail bouncing.

I sighed. "Oh my God, she's so cute."

Holden sighed right back. "Oh my God, he's so handsome."

I followed his gaze to see a group of football players tossing a ball. Oliver was in the group, smiling. I pursed my lips. "Guess being a good field goal kicker gets you past the racists."

My best friend elbowed me in the ribs.

"Ow."

"Keep your voice down." He hush-whispered the words.

"What? You're worried the racists might have their feelings—"

"Oh, for fuck's sake, shut the hell up," he snapped back at me.

I eyed him. "Oh."

"Yeah, *oh*." He rolled his eyes.

"You *like* him." I extended the *like* in that way guaranteed to annoy the shit out of him.

"We established that last night." He glanced over at Mr. Janz, our music teacher, but he was busy with percussion. At least they weren't pounding on their drums at the moment. Holden pivoted his attention back to me. "Why don't you just ask her out? What's the worst that can happen?"

"She says no?" I shot him my patented *duh* look.

"So what if she does?"

"Then…" I scrunched my nose. Everyone in school already knew I was out, so she couldn't out me again. "She might…think less of me…"

"Good Lord." He set his trumpet down and then turned toward me. "And what if she says *yes*? Has that ever occurred to you? You're a catch—"

"I'm short, compact, and dress like a butch."

He winced. "Okay, I didn't say that as an insult, and I'm sorry you took it as such."

"Yeah, well, I'm sorry about the *style* comment." I pursed my lips again. "Well, a little bit sorry."

"You're getting off track."

Because I don't like the track we're on? I want off…

"She might say *yes*. She might look at you and think *there's someone I want to spend my time with*."

This time, I rolled my eyes. "She's tall, gorgeous, and straight."

"Maybe…" He tapped his lips with his index finger. "First, what if she's queer?"

I tried to speak, but he held up his hand.

Annoyed—but intrigued—I desisted.

"We don't know who is and isn't queer."

"Well, have you seen the new ninth grader? Michael something…"

"You can't tell by looks, but yeah, I noticed him. If anyone gives him a hard time, we'll stand up for him."

I grinned. "See? Even you can learn—"

"By calling Principal Kouriki and then beating a hasty retreat. I don't want to get hurt. I don't want you to get hurt. That's a thing. We've avoided it so far. Shall we survive high school without a black eye or a chipped tooth?"

"You could trip and fall on your trumpet and chip your—"

"Focus."

I huffed.

He grinned. "She doesn't seem like she'd be insulted if you asked her out."

"Holden?"

"Hmm?"

"We've been in the same class as Juliette since ninth grade."

"What's your point?" He eyed me.

"That if she was gay, bi, or pan, we would've found out by now."

He snickered. "If you hadn't been caught kissing Susan, would you have come out? I only remember seeing you with guys."

"Uh…"

"Right. And since I didn't want the hassle—or for anyone to give Mom a hard time—I was planning on staying in my roomy walk-in closet until I escaped to university."

Huh. And okay, sure, Juliette might be doing the same, but what were the odds? One in twenty? I wasn't going to make a fool of myself with that kind of probability.

"Hey, it's Holden, right? And Peyton."

A smooth voice caught me off guard, and if Holden's look of surprise was genuine, he hadn't heard anyone approaching either.

I turned to find Oliver behind us. He wore a sweat-soaked T-shirt and shorts. Appropriate clothing on this humid night. Fall was still a long way off. Closer to the next game, though, the guys would wear their practice gear. I liked the way his clothes clung to those muscles. His pink cheeks added to the pretty picture.

"Uh…" Holden's jaw opened and closed several times.

God help me. A little prayer never hurt. "You're Oliver, right?" I waved in the direction of the other players, some of whom were sitting on the ground and drinking from their water bottles. "You're taking…a time-out?"

He grinned. "Yeah."

I blinked. No one had the right to have such perfect teeth, such a wide smile, and…just a sense of genuineness about him. I didn't detect anything but a quiet happiness. My empathic insight didn't always work, but this guy was pretty easy to read. And as attractive as I found him, I still glanced over his shoulder to catch sight of the cheerleaders all crowded in a circle. I refocused on Oliver. "Kicker?"

He wiped his brow with his forearm, showing off some impressive biceps. "Yeah."

"Fifty-nine yards?"

His expression turned rueful as he shrugged. "I had a tailwind, so it wouldn't have really counted toward a record or—"

"The longest field goal ever kicked in high school was sixty-eight yards." Holden said the words super-fast.

Both Oliver and I turned to my friend.

He turned a pleasant shade of puce.

Oliver recovered first. "That's right. Thirty-five years later and the record still stands. As you can see, I was off that—"

"Yes, but you would've tied the North Carolina record." Again word vomited.

Sheesh. We get it. You can use a search engine.

"But neither of those guys had a tailwind." Oliver scratched his cheek. A cheek with just the lightest touch of stubble. "At least I think they didn't."

I managed to snag Holden's hand before he successfully reached for his cell phone. "We'll go with *doesn't matter* and agree you're amazing. Right,

Holden?" I gave him my most winsome smile while telegraphing *you're being an idiot*.

Oliver cleared his throat. "I just…I came to thank you. Both." He was quick to wave between Holden and myself.

I wasn't certain my *friend* had done that much. Well, he'd stood next to me. Or sort of behind me. Effort counted, right?

Oliver's gaze kept straying to Holden.

"You're welcome." I grinned.

"We d-didn't do anything," Holden stammered.

Oliver cocked his head. "You stood up for me. You defended me. Hell, you don't even know me."

"No, but we'd like to get to know you better." I nudged Holden.

Who just continued to gawk.

I stuck out my hand for formal introductions. "Peyton Morris."

"I'm Oliver Barton. From Oregon. That seems to have been the most frequently asked question of me today—and there have been a lot."

His grip was solid and yet not overpowering. I liked that. "We don't get a lot of newcomers. Occasionally, we get kids whose parents commute to Raleigh, but it's really too far. We're quite isolated up here in the mountains. Unless your uncle works at the factory? Or your aunt? Holden's mother does, on the shop floor no less. She's super capable and—"

"Holden Whittle." He held out his hand.

Oliver shook it.

Ha. Knew if I started talking about his personal life that he'd intervene. Go, me!

"Nice to meet you, Holden." Then, as if realizing

he'd been shaking hands a bit too long, Oliver released Holden's hand. He turned to me. "And you too, Peyton."

I grinned. He ticked a bunch of my boxes, but he wasn't slender, brown-haired, and a cheerleader. I peeked over Oliver's shoulder again and— "Oh shit." I tried to duck behind him. Well, put him in front of me. And hide me because this wasn't happening and—

"Hey, Juliette, how's it going? Lovely to see you." Holden's kind words dripped just a touch. Only so much that I'd notice because we'd been friends for a million years. "Peyton's happy to see you. She was just remarking how good the squad looks this year."

Slowly, I raised my gaze from Oliver's chest to meet the one of the young woman who'd come to stand beside him.

Dark-brown eyes, crinkled in evident amusement, met mine. "Nice to see you, Peyton." Juliette nudged Oliver. "I met this guy at Lou's Diner last night and hadn't had a chance to say *hi* all day."

"You missed the kerfuffle this morning." Oliver winced, glancing over at his teammates.

"No." Juliette shook her head. "I saw the whole thing." First she touched Holden's biceps, then she stroked mine.

Oh my God, she's touching me. I hadn't given her permission, but I so didn't care at that moment.

"These two are fearless. Always have been." Juliette gazed between Holden and me.

Holden snorted.

We all turned to him.

He cleared his throat. "Uh, I was trying to drag Peyton out of there. She was the one who wanted to take each of those assholes down." He winced. "Sorry."

Oliver frowned. "Why? Juliette was right. You were fear—"

"He's apologizing for swearing in front of me." Juliette chuckled. "I've told him a thousand times that it doesn't bother me. If it did, I wouldn't have survived high school so far."

"Uh…" Oliver blinked. "You don't swear?"

Juliette shook her head. Her ponytail swished a little. She offered a serene smile. "My parents are firm about me making a good impression. They believe curse words diminish a person's standing."

"I read that people who swear have higher IQs." Holden frowned. "Or was it that they had larger vocabularies? Fuck me, I can't remember and shit—" He clapped a hand over his mouth. From behind it, he uttered, "Sorry."

A hearty laugh came from Juliette. "Oh, Holden, you give my life more color." She met my gaze. "Like…all the colors of the rainbow." She pivoted to Oliver. "I meant they're brave because they're both out and, dare I say, proud. A real inspiration for other kids."

I pretended to look around. "I don't exactly see the masses coming out to join us." *Ouch. Maybe a touch too much sarcasm.*

She shrugged. "You don't know where a kid might be on their journey. Watching you be out, they might find the strength to tell their parents. Or they might just be able to admit it to themselves. Or they might be too scared for either, but they see what can be, and one day that might be them." She turned back to Oliver. "This town is pretty friendly, like I told you yesterday. You met…some of the…less nice kids this morning. You just need to stay away from them, and you'll be fine." She glanced over uneasily. "Except the ones on your team. Sorry about them."

"When they heard I could kick, they decided to be less of the fuckwits they'd been this morning. Well, Gary hasn't apologized."

"He plays lacrosse." I scowled.

Oliver tilted his head.

"It's a given the football players would apologize— Coach will eat them alive if they pull that shit around him. Hell, they were playing with fire even doing what they did this morning. If I'd told Coach…" *Huh. I totally should've told him. Damn. Except that would've endangered his spot on the team, which would have in turn endangered me. I would've been playing with fire. Maybe the right thing to do, but not the thing that would keep me alive and in one piece.*

"I'm glad you didn't." Oliver's smile reached his eyes. "This is a good team, and I'm lucky to be joining it. Yeah, it sucks they were assholes this morning. But they've been decent ever since."

"Gary's really the ringleader," Holden offered. "But that doesn't exonerate Larry and Dominic for following."

I nudged him. "Exonerate's a big word."

He flushed a cute pink.

Suddenly, Juliette's discomfort when referring to the other football players sank in. "What kids do you need to avoid?" Most of the shit seemed to pass right over Juliette since she was the captain of the award-winning cheer squad.

Unless I'd been wrong.

Well, duh. "Who's been picking on you? What have they been saying? Tell me who, and I'll…I'll…hit 'em over the head with my clarinet."

Holden snorted.

I glared.

Juliette brushed her fingers along my biceps.

Little butterflies fluttered in my belly. Funny, I didn't remember her being touchy-feely before. Maybe this was Oliver's influence? His entire demeanor screamed *fun-loving guy*.

Juliette giggled. "You're so sweet."

A whistle blew.

"Oh, that's me. Gotta go." With a little wave, she sauntered away.

Oliver watched her. *Is he checking out her ass?* Those short skirts didn't leave much to the imagination. Which might've been why I was staring at her sturdy thighs and remembering her cute butt when she wore those tight jeans and her perky breasts when she wore that tight T-shirt and—

"Yeah, shit, I gotta go as well. Back to practice." Oliver, who'd apparently stopped staring at Juliette's ass and was now staring at Holden, grinned. "I'll see you tomorrow, right?"

"Mr. Santos's Spanish class. Every afternoon."

Before Holden could say anything stupider, Oliver took off at a run toward the field where the team was huddled.

Holden sighed.

I whacked him on the chest.

Playfully.

He glared and pivoted to me, seemingly to shake himself out of his little stupidity trance. "What the hell was that, Peyton? You'll hit them with your clarinet? You're so lame."

"Well, better than *Mr. Santos's Spanish class every afternoon…*"

Holden swiped his trumpet off the ground and glared.

I glared back.

As always, he broke first. "Yeah, okay." He offered a small smile. "Juliette was friendly."

Feeling like I was walking on stars, I buffed my clarinet with the tail of my shirt. "She said I was *sweet*." I sighed.

Much like Holden had.

"Best day ever."

"For you, maybe. I made an ass of myself."

I smacked his gut. "You've got the entire semester of Spanish to make up for it. I'm sure you'll be whispering sweet nothings *en Español* to each other in no time."

"He's straight, Pey. I don't try to convert guys. Not my jam."

Remembering the looks Oliver had been giving Holden, I smacked him again. "Never say never."

Mr. Janz clapped his hands, clearly—finally—finished with percussion.

With everything that had happened today, I was ready to call it a day. Instead, I prepared to play "The Star-Spangled Banner."

Chapter Four

Oliver

I was ready to drop dead when I slid into Uncle Jeremiah's car at the end of practice.

Instead of jeering, several of the other players waved to me and my uncle. He and my aunt were new in town, so these kids didn't know them. In fact, when I'd left Lake Oswego, I'd thought I was moving to Washington, DC. Uncle Jeremiah got the transfer order within days of my arrival, and the next thing I knew, we were headed to North Carolina. Not a long car ride, but a shit ton of distance between here and DC. Culturally, at least. With his government job, though, he went wherever they told him to.

Aunt Leslie, my mother's sister, enjoyed her vocation as a school teacher. She'd been snapped up by Pinedale's board of education and now taught second grade in the elementary school.

"How're you doing?" Uncle Jeremiah pulled the car out of the lot and onto the street.

"I could've walked home."

"I know you could." Amusement laced his voice. "But Leslie's got book club—some feminist book she's insisting I read—"

"Which you will." I smiled.

"Ah, you know me well. I will definitely read it. For

the sake of my marriage and also because that author writes really great books that I love. I'm a full supporter of women's rights." He headed us toward downtown.

"Are we going to Lou's Diner?"

"Yeah. I figured you'd be hungry."

I was exhausted, but we hadn't had much time together since moving to town. He'd done a series of seminars in Raleigh and would get home late every night and be gone before dawn. I thought that was brutal work, but Aunt Leslie accidentally told me the salary he made. Yeah, I'd put in crazy hours for that kind of money too. When I asked her what he did exactly, she got super vague. I chalked it up to her thinking I was still a kid. They'd barely seen me since my parents died and I lived in Oregon with my grandmother. My dad's mother. Who was now in a nursing home. I'd wanted to get a little apartment and stay near her for my final year of high school, but everyone nixed that idea. No emancipation for me.

"Uh, I am hungry." My sluggish mind could barely keep up.

"You okay?" He parked on the street. "We can always go home."

"Nah, we're here now." I unbuckled my seat belt and offered my biggest smile. I didn't like thinking about how my grandmother was sliding farther and farther into the past with her Alzheimer's. Many days, she'd mistake me for my dad. I'd been prepared to take care of her, but she had chest pains one day, and I'd called an ambulance. The diagnosis of congestive heart failure, added to the clear Alzheimer's, earned my grandma a nice nursing home where they could take care of her properly.

I got out of the car and glanced up and down the

main street. A few couples strolled, but that was it. Given the late hour—and the fact today had been the first day of school—I figured most of the kids were home in bed.

Morgan greeted us as soon as we stepped in the door. "My buddy Oliver." They grinned. Today they wore grunge jeans, combat boots, and a sweatshirt with holes in the elbows and frayed sleeves. Still wearing the apron which, I'd figured out, was the uniform.

"Hi, Morgan. This is my uncle, Jeremiah."

Their megawatt smile warmed me a little. I always worried about my Black uncle. Shouldn't have to…but did. Of course, Morgan's treatment of Juliette yesterday had given me the notion we'd be welcome.

"Booth at the back?" Morgan leaned in. "We've got a pile of kids from the high school, and they're in a rowdy mood. They'll behave, of course." They glanced at Jeremiah. "Martha boots people who don't behave, and they're never allowed back."

"Somewhere quiet would be nice." Jeremiah offered just as sincere a grin. "Loud doesn't appeal to me tonight. Unless…" He met my gaze.

I shook my head. *No thank you. No rowdy teenagers tonight.*

Morgan guided us to a booth near the door to the kitchen but, mercifully, away from all the noise. I slid in as Morgan presented us with menus.

Before I could thank them, they tapped the table. "I love this song."

Over the din of both the kitchen and teenagers a few booths over, I had to listen carefully to pick out the song. Personally, I loved they didn't blast the music here. When I came into an establishment like this, I wanted to hear the person I was with as well as myself being able to think. As I identified the song, I met Morgan's grin. "Yeah, I love this song. Her best, I think."

They leaned in. "We're not supposed to admit liking someone this popular. Dorky, if you know what I mean."

I tilted my head. I'd never thought of it that way. If I liked a singer or band, I just enjoyed them. "So I'm supposed to pretend I don't like her? Because she's so damned talented? Versatile?"

Morgan shrugged. "I say to own it." They indicated their clothes. "You can see I couldn't give two shits about what other people think." They glanced toward Jeremiah. "Oops."

My uncle laughed. "First, cursing doesn't bother me"—he slanted me a glance—"but it might other people."

Aunt Leslie.

"Second, I own this album. Her best yet. Very different from her other stuff—which I also own all of."

Morgan laughed, then tapped our menus. "I'll be back in a few to grab your orders." They eyed me. "Cola?"

I shook my head. "Ginger ale? I have to sleep tonight."

"I'll take one also." Jeremiah met my gaze. "Another early morning for me as well."

"Great. Be right back." Morgan headed toward the counter. The soda machine was behind it. They playfully nudged a young woman as they went, then gently smacked a loud dude on the back of the head. I read it as a *simmer down* gesture. Certainly not meant to injure or embarrass.

Morgan left me with the impression they liked touching—with permission. I wasn't used to that. "They are…very cheerful."

Jeremiah grinned. "Yes, they are."

"So you're okay with…" I waved.

"Yeah." His smile reached his eyes. "In my profession, we're taught acceptance—because we encounter all kinds of people in our work. Some of my coworkers snicker at our training, but I think it makes us better at our jobs. I don't understand Morgan's identity—but I can recognize their right to be themselves. Who am I to say what they should do?"

I swallowed a lump in my throat. "I suppose I should tell you about my day." His simple acceptance of queer folk warmed my heart. "I met some kids."

Jeremiah opened the menu but held my gaze. "I sort of figured that would happen on your first day of school."

A laugh burst from me. A genuine expression of amusement. "Well, yeah, see, that's the thing."

He held up his hands and perused the menu, running his finger up and down the plastic carefully. "Okay, I know what I want. Do you?"

I nodded.

"Great. Now, tell me about these kids."

I cleared my throat. "I'll start with the nice ones."

He arched an eyebrow. "I'm not certain I like the sound of this, but go ahead."

After long consideration, I sighed. *I owe him the whole truth.* So I started with the hard ones. "Well, this group of guys saw me get out of your car…" The insults they'd hurled at me—and by extension, my uncle—still hurt. I'd never heard such horrible things. Aunt Leslie had once, casually, suggested I'd been protected in my corner of Oregon. I hadn't believed her.

Now I did.

By the time I finished the clean version of the insults, Morgan had arrived, taken our food order, and departed. I was having a cheeseburger—since they were, apparently, the best in town. My uncle had chosen a grilled chicken salad. I'd done my best not to wince guiltily. I should've been more concerned about eating healthy, but my metabolism and the crazy training schedule for football meant I could indulge in a greasy satisfying burger with a side of sautéed mushroom and onion rings on occasion.

Plus, I'd had a bad day.

"No physical altercation?" Jeremiah looked me over as if trying to figure out if I had injuries I hadn't shared. I was a little sore from football practice—but that came from not have worked out intensely for a couple of weeks during the chaos of the move. I'd been for a few runs, but we'd just set up the gym equipment my aunt and uncle insisted on buying for me.

"No." I winced. "We didn't get to that point." Slowly, as the memory assailed me, I managed a smile. "A pint-sized purple-haired girl…woman… I'm not sure. Anyway, I found out later her name's Peyton, and she charged in there, and…" I sought the right words. "She started pointing out things about the bullies. Like one has a sister married to a Black man and how she—Peyton—would call his sister and repeat some of the things he'd said."

Jeremiah chuckled.

"And I don't know…I didn't understand everything, but man, she was a powder keg. I'd worried about the guys exploding, but she looked ready to blow too. And then—" I had to slow down and find the right words. "—

her friend intervened. Tried to cool things down. I think, if she'd been in danger, he would've tried to pull her out. Or fight himself. He's half a foot taller than her and half a foot shorter than me." At six-one, having gone through a brutal growth spurt last year, I towered over many of the other kids. Awkwardly. Fortunately, all the changes hadn't thrown off my kicking skills.

"They sound brave."

I nodded furiously. "They are. They're—"

"I've got your food." Morgan gave me a quick glance as they put the food on the table. "Ketchup's there. Can I get you anything else?"

My salivary glands worked overtime as I sniffed the aroma of grease, meat, and the best food substance on the planet. I doubted my uncle would let me get away with eating mushrooms for every meal. Too bad. "This looks amazing."

Jeremiah picked up his fork. "Yes, please thank the chef."

Morgan arched an eyebrow. "I'll thank our line cook. I doubt he'll appreciate it."

I wasn't going to try to unpack that. Every time I went to a food establishment—with either my aunt, my uncle, or both—they offered their thanks both to the waitstaff as well as the cook or chef or whomever. This wasn't something I was accustomed to, but I liked it. Yeah, I'd feel silly, but that person slaved over a hot stove to bring me delicious food. Or served that food while being on their feet all day. My thanks was the least I could do.

Morgan departed, and Jeremiah caught my gaze. "My mother was a waitress for nearly forty years. They call them servers now. Anyway, she worked so hard and put me through college—along with a couple of scholarships and grants. I wanted to pay her back, but she died in her sleep just after I graduated. The doctor said she had a stroke. Just like that." He snapped his fingers. Then pointed to my food. "Before it goes cold."

Needing no further encouragement, I dug in. I didn't remember anyone ever talking about my great-aunt. Or something. By marriage. I was still sorting these things out. Aunt Leslie was much younger than my mother, and while she'd stayed on the East Coast, my mother had gone west for college. At the University of Portland, she'd earned a PhD in education while she and my dad were raising me. She'd graduated a couple of years before they both died in the crash. One thing I'd known, even at thirteen, was how badly they wanted more kids. I'd overheard the problem was something with Mom. And that Aunt Leslie had the same condition, and that's why she hadn't had a child either.

I didn't know the details and wasn't about to ask. Even if Aunt Leslie and Uncle Jeremiah wanted children, I was pretty sure a seventeen-year-old nephew wouldn't have been their first choice.

"That must be a good burger." Jeremiah pointed.

I had to swallow before responding. "Yeah."

"You seem lost in thought. Are you thinking about those two young people who intervened?"

No, but that's a good change of topic. A topic you didn't even know about. "Sort of. I found out Peyton was, I think, one of the first girls to come out as bisexual in our class. A couple of years ago. Something about being filmed while kissing a girl under the bleachers."

"That might be illegal."

"The kid who shared the recording got in huge

trouble, and everyone had to remove it from their phones." But the internet was forever. That video was probably out there somewhere.

"You need to be careful." My uncle speared a piece of lettuce. "You're off to university in a year. Staying out of trouble is a good idea."

"I know." He'd mentioned this before. As had Aunt Leslie. As had my parents when I was younger. Everyone seemed convinced I was going to get in some sort of trouble.

Uncle Jeremiah put down his fork. "Your cousin's in jail. Deservedly. But I know he didn't need to go looking for trouble. Trouble found him. Your other two cousins are studying hard and trying to…" He winced.

Even if he deserved punishment for something he'd done wrong, I understood how tough life could be after jail. Our neighbor back in Lake Oswego had served time for marijuana offenses from the early eighties. Had messed up his life—coming out of jail with a record. Now that pot was legal, he was working on getting a pardon. Or something. Or maybe it would be automatic. I wasn't certain. I just knew he'd had a tough time finding a good job over the years.

Jeremiah sighed. "I want the best for them. For you. That means staying away from trouble. That means staying away from fights."

"I didn't start it."

"No, but that rarely matters. I mean, defend yourself if you must, but walk away whenever you can. Better that than the alternative."

"Won't kids think I'm a coward?"

"Who cares what they think? They won't have an impact on your future—a record will."

I flashed to Holden—all shaggy brown hair, soulful brown eyes, and a dorky sense of humor. He and Peyton competed for who was more sarcastic.

Jeremiah swallowed a bite. "Okay, you have to share."

I cocked my head.

"You've stopped eating, and you just got the goofiest grin on your face." He gave me what I thought of as his pensive expression. Like he was having a deep conversation with himself. Compared to him and Aunt Leslie, I felt shallow. Like I didn't have their perspective on the world.

"Just…you remember I talked about Peyton?"

"The spitfire? She sounds like a good person. Like someone you might befriend."

"Yeah. Well, her guy friend stepped in as well. Holden." *Don't blush.* "He also seems like a nice guy. They play in the marching band. She's clarinet, and he's trumpet."

"So you'll see them often. That's great."

I wasn't going to dig in to that. "And I also met the captain of the cheer squad. Her name's Juliette. She's in my AP English and physics classes. Holden's in my Spanish class." I stuck my fork into a mushroom. "He came out as gay after the video of Peyton became public. He's…" *Cute? Brave? Bold?* "A good guy."

"That's good. That you can be friends with these people. Just…"

"Stay out of trouble?"

Jeremiah grinned. "I was going to say eat your mushrooms."

He wasn't. But that was okay. I knew what he meant. I knew what I had to do.

Chapter Five

Juliette

"You staring at me is super annoying." I tried to focus on the math problem that had me stymied. My unusual companion was, by his own admission, useless in this department.

Duncan bristled, opening and closing his mouth several times. "I'm not accustomed to being spoken to like that."

I snickered. "You're not accustomed to being spoken to by anyone, you mean."

He frowned. "That is accurate."

I met his gaze. "Look, dude, I'm as confused as you. Given how long you've been hanging around, I'm not clear why I'm the first person you've been able to converse with."

"You're the first person who's ever seen me. Or at least has admitted to it."

Snorting, I suppressed a laugh. "I'm certain if someone else had spotted you, they would've spoken up." I used my pencil to size him up. "The uniform gives you away."

He straightened in the seat in the row across from me. I'd snuck into Mrs. Bletchley's classroom for lunch period so I could get some extra study on my math problems. Calculus, no less. The bane of my existence.

But if I wanted med school, I needed perfect grades. My mom was a gerontologist working in Pinedale and several other small towns near us. Dad was the CEO of a biotech firm in Chapel Hill. My brother graduated at the top of his class here at Pinedale three years ago, and now Charlie was at Harvard doing his darn best to get into the law school there. He didn't have access to a legacy spot, so he'd just have to work his tush off. His straight A-pluses last year were helping him get noticed.

"What's wrong with my uniform?"

I sighed. I was skipping lunch with the squad to study. Now I was having an in-depth discussion with a ghost. A ghost who, apparently, only I could see. "Well, you said it's from the Civil War."

"I fought for the Union."

"Right." I did some quick math in my head. "You were in the Battle of Boykin's Mill. That was one hundred and sixty years ago."

"True."

I gazed at him, but he wouldn't meet my eye. He never did when discussing this aspect of the war. We were in the second week of school, and for reasons I couldn't explain, I'd been able to *see* Duncan for the past two weeks. Funny that in my previous three years at the school, he'd never appeared.

"Maybe I can see you because it's some kind of anniversary?"

Duncan finally met my gaze. "Of a sort."

"Didn't the war end not long after the battle?" I'd studied history, but I hadn't immersed myself in the wars as some of my classmates had. I'd tried for a larger overview of world history and geography rather than the nitty-gritty of any one encounter. And I should've gone diving into the internet to figure this all out. But…I kind of liked pulling it out of him a bit at a time. Plus, between all my classes, cheering, and brutal calculus, I was pretty busy. That lack of curiosity about history didn't stand me in good stead in life. I just hadn't cared.

Much to the annoyance of my ninth-grade American History teacher.

"Did you die at the battle?"

"No."

I put my pencil down and swiveled in my seat to see him better. "But you died in 1865."

"Yes."

I closed my right eye as I wracked my brain. "Did you die of an infection? Some kind of wound? Consumption or diphtheria or something like that? Lots of nasty things going around. Personally, I'm grateful for vaccines. Whooping cough sounds horrendous."

"I did not die of an illness, and I wish to change the subject."

"That's fine with me." I spun, picked up my pencil, and tried to focus on first principle. Nothing in algebra or statistics had prepared me for this foreign language. I sighed.

"What is wrong? You've been sighing greatly since I've known you."

I turned my gaze back to him.

He cleared his throat. "Well, since I truly noticed you. I saw you around the school before, of course, but…" He straightened his uniform. "We hadn't spoken."

"Have you ever spoken to anyone who isn't a ghost?"

"No." He said the word with an odd finality.

"So you've been wandering the halls since the first school was built at the turn of the last century, and I'm the first person you've been able to materialize to meet?"

"Since the inception…" He scrunched his nose. "Well, I've been on this plot of land for all my spectral existence. That's the correct term?"

I waved my hand. "You know way more than I do about this stuff. Did they even have that word back then?"

He pursed his lips. "I admit to only hearing it in the last forty or fifty years."

"Forty or fifty…"

He blinked.

"I just wonder what life will be like when I can casually mention that much time. I mean, I've changed a lot since I was seven."

"We all change every day." He nodded. "Yes, I can see how childhood to adulthood is a great upheaval. Great transformation."

"You use lots of big words."

"You speak well yourself," he challenged right back. "Not this…slang…that I hear from most of the students."

I winced. "My parents are professionals. Like, important people. My mom cares for old people—as a doctor—and my dad employs hundreds of people. Who, in turn, take care of their families and loved ones. Rippling out, both my parents have huge impacts on those around them."

"And you feel that you do not?"

"I'm captain of the cheer squad."

"That requires discipline."

"And I was lucky they chose me."

"Why do you say that? Were you not the most qualified?"

His comment made me wonder how much he actually knew about what went on in the school. I held up my hands. "Uh…Black…"

"As am I."

"And that didn't impact you? Growing up in the 1840s and '50s?"

"Well, I was in a Negro reconnaissance group. Contrabands, they called us. Escaped slaves who were often sent out on scouting missions during the war. A few of my friends were even spies."

He'd piqued my interest, so I closed my textbook. *Calculus can wait.*

"Scouting? Spies?" I sat straighter. "Were you an escaped slave? How did you get away? What happened to your family?"

"I do not wish to discuss it. We were having a discourse about your sighs."

At times, his vocabulary appeared vast. Had he been educated, or had he simply absorbed more than a hundred years of other people speaking? I wanted to know, but he'd effectively closed that door. *For today.* I'd take up the *discourse* again. He and his past were way more interesting than calculus.

"Well, I'm remembering something that happened last week."

"And it still distresses you?"

"Racism will always distress me. Just good old-fashioned racism." I winced.

"Directed toward you?"

I shook my head and blew out a breath. "No, not me. Other kids are less likely to say something because I'm the cheer captain. So I'm pretty lucky. And my teammates would get super mad. You do not want to be ostracized by the most popular girls in the school. Let's be honest—they can be vicious."

"But not you?"

"No." I eyed my painted fingernails. My mom wouldn't let me get fake nails, even over the summer when I didn't have cheer practice. If I ever got out from under her and quit cheering, I planned to get some. "I have to be, as my parents would say, *above the fray*."

He squinted.

"*Above reproach.*" I tapped my fingers on my textbook. "They use lots of big words too. Of course, I understand them. I read lots of adult books during the summer as well as taking several AP classes in summer school. I wanted a job, but working in a shop at the mall or at Lou's Diner would've taken up *precious time*." I used air quotes.

After a moment, he chuckled. "They want the best for you."

"Which would be why I have to pass calculus."

"What incident occurred? When you witnessed this racism?"

"Just…a bunch of…jerks. They went after the new White kid because he was dropped off at school by a Black man who is, in fact, Oliver's uncle."

"Oliver is the boy who was bullied?"

I disliked *boy* and *girl* even though I used them myself. Well, boys sometimes got guys, which was way cool because that didn't give away their age. Nothing like that for girls, though. Girl or woman. Nothing in between. Maybe gals, but we rarely used that word. But we were teenagers. On the cusp of adulthood. *Young women* and *young men* and *young enbies*. Unfortunately, adults still saw us all as children.

And jerks like Larry, Dominic, and Gary didn't help us rise in adults' estimation of us. "Yeah, Oliver was bullied." I tilted my head. "How old are you? Because you don't look—"

"We are not discussing me. We are discussing what occurred to your friend Oliver."

"You can't be more than twenty-five. Thirty?"

He pressed his lips together, and his jaw ticked. After a moment, he supplied, "Twenty."

"Huh?" Okay, that I hadn't seen coming. He was practically my age, but he carried…an air of authority. Of wisdom. Of knowledge. Like he'd lived a hard life. *He was an escaped slave who fought in a war. What did you think? That life had been a breeze for him?* "Sorry, twenty."

"And Oliver…was he assaulted? I hadn't heard anything, but then I don't always."

I shook my head. "Nope. Peyton and Holden intervened."

"Peyton and Holden?" He gazed upward, brow furrowed.

Is he thinking really hard? At times, over the past two weeks, I was almost certain I understood him. Then he'd say or do something that made me realize I was often clueless.

"These people are White?"

"Yes."

"In my day, Black and White never mixed."

I thought about all my White friends. And all my Black friends. And all my Hispanic, Indian, and South Asian friends. My school wasn't as diverse as, say, a school in Raleigh or Chapel Hill might be, but we had kids from a number of different backgrounds. As well as all my gay and straight friends. The reasons why guys like those three bozos drove me nuts. They risked giving our school a bad reputation. The wrong reputation. "That's really sad. I mean, there are still people who believe schools should be segregated, but that's…" *No, you can't say* bullshit. *Mom would kill you.* "Uh, unfortunate."

He raised an eyebrow. "I'm certain there's another word for it. This school has been integrated for as long as I can remember. A hard-won victory."

"And the right thing to do."

"I have a question."

"Only one?"

"Don't get smart with me." He said it with an authoritative tone…mixed with a bit of amusement.

I smiled.

He continued. "You say this boy is White."

Had I? "Yes."

"And his uncle is Black."

"Yes." *Where's he going with this?*

"I find it strange that a Black man would be allowed to fall in love with a White woman and then marry her."

"Uh, you know interracial marriage has been legal…" I wracked my brain, but I couldn't remember the year of that Supreme Court decision. One of the good ones. "Everyone should be able to fall in love and marry whomever they want." I was firm about this. Still, I contemplated my odd companion. "Have you ever been in love?"

"No." Definitive. Certain. Harsh.

I didn't think he was telling the truth for even one

second. "You never had a crush? Perhaps on a White lady…" *Was he in love once? And it was forbidden? That would be sad.* Especially since he'd died so young.

"No. I would never allow my feelings to develop like that. With someone inappropriate."

"You can't just turn off your feelings like that, Duncan. If you truly care about someone, then you…have to find a way to show them."

"Actually, you can turn them off. You must. You have to." Again, with the *I'm not messing around* attitude.

"Well, what if I don't want to?" *Ha. I can give a little attitude right back.*

This time, his stare unnerved just a little bit.

"Who do you…have a crush on? Is that the right word? Or is this love?"

I almost bit my nail, only catching myself at the last moment. "Uh…someone I shouldn't."

"Why? Because they're the wrong color?"

I slumped in my seat. "Yes. Well, that's part of it. My parents are proud Black people. They've worked hard to give me everything, and that's amazing. I'm appreciative, right?" I sighed. "But they want me to be perfect. I'm tired of being perfect."

"Ah."

Duncan's dark-brown eyes mesmerized me as he clearly thought out his next words.

"And falling in love with someone who is the wrong color isn't *perfect*?"

"If he was rich, successful, and handsome, I think it might be okay with my parents. But if the person…isn't like that…I don't think they'd be happy. And the person I *have a crush on*"—again with the air quotes—"isn't like that. Isn't like me. They're…just not who I think my parents would want for me. Everyone thinks I'm dating Lucas. He's the captain of the football team and the quarterback. He's also so not my type."

"How?"

"It doesn't matter."

"But there is someone else. Someone who isn't, as you say, *perfect.*" He appeared to consider. "Pride is hard to swallow. I had to join an all-Negro regiment because my skin was Black. We were paid less. We had to pay for our uniforms. Some White officers fought against those unjust regulations, but nothing changed. Still, I wanted to fight for the Union, so I accepted lower pay and fought with my heart and soul."

"I'm sorry. That was awful for you. First you're a slave. Then you escape slavery. Then you fight with an army that treats you badly. Finally, you die. That…sucks. But today's better." I had to find some kind of silver lining for what he'd fought and died for. "We have interracial marriage. We have same-sex marriage. We have freedoms you could only have imagined of. And most importantly—and I'm certain you've noticed—we don't have slavery."

"But it's not been abolished everywhere yet, has it?"

Damn. "No, there are different kinds of slaves in other countries, and that's super sad. We've got social justice warriors, but they can only do so much. As long as horrible people are in charge, changing things is difficult."

"That's an interesting comment."

Which I was neither going to elaborate on nor unpack.

"With all that progress, though, you are still afraid

of loving the wrong person?"

"Yes." That simple. Truly.

Duncan sighed. "Me too."

That had me sitting up straight. "You mean ghosts fall in love?"

He gave me an amused, crooked smile. "I'm not the only ghost around here. Sometimes we even talk. There's this other ghost who is…what do you kids say? Ah, *cool.*"

I wasn't certain anyone said *cool* these days.

"I would like to get to know them better, but they always run and hide."

"Oh, that's…crappy." What was a little swear word between friends?

"Yes, as you say."

"Sucks to be us."

"As you say."

The end-of-lunch bell rang. I gathered my books and shoved them in my backpack. *So much for learning first principle.* "Nice talking to you. I won't be here tomorrow because the cheer squad is doing a demonstration over the lunch period. Out on the field. You should come and watch."

Duncan offered an enigmatic smile. "I just might. Goodbye, Juliette."

"Bye, Duncan." Before he could answer, I exited the room.

Chapter Six

Willie

Unspeakable excitement rocketed through me when I spotted Holden entering the library. I tracked him until he sat at an isolated desk near the history section. European Renaissance, no less. *Pretty safe bet we won't be disturbed.* "Psst."

His head shot up, the harsh overhead lights hitting his brown hair in this cute way that almost derailed me.

He gazed over to the stacks and narrowed his eyes as he scanned the small space between the top of the books and the row above.

After a long moment, he clearly spotted me as his mouth broke into a huge grin and his adorable brown eyes sparkled with amusement. "I assume you still don't have clothes?"

I puffed out my chest. Then deflated. "Uh, no."

He laughed. "You know, my offer to find you actual clothes stands. You're naked in the library again. Is this some kind of fetish? You want to go around flashing people in second period? It's been almost three weeks. Which is kind of weird."

Has he figured it out yet? He seems clever, but maybe he doesn't really believe. And of course, I didn't go around *flashing* people.

He continued. "We've had a couple of football

games—"

I sighed.

He pivoted to face me. "What's with the sigh?"

"Just…football players…"

"Tell me about it." He groaned.

"What's up?" That was a phrase that carried through generations.

"I'm in love with a straight guy."

This time, I chuckled. "Oh dear, that is a dilemma. May I assume he's a football player?"

Holden's gaze shot around, but this early in the morning—with the library just having opened—we were alone. Plus…European Renaissance history… "Yeah. A straight football player."

"And you're gay."

"Right. Didn't we have this discussion?"

"We did. I'm simply confirming that facts haven't changed since the last time we spoke."

"I didn't straighten out, if that's what you're thinking." He grinned. "Of course, Peyton wants me to wear glitter in my hair this week. I think she's crazy. That shit gets everywhere." He tapped his pen on his Spanish textbook. "She thinks, because she knows I won't do that, that I should put on some sparkly eyeshadow."

I blinked. "Well, that would be interesting. Do men wear makeup?"

"Sure. All the time." He frowned. "Okay, like, more on television than in our town. Peyton thinks I should be *showier*."

"What do you think?"

"That I can be gay and not wear eyeliner. That someone else can and it's totally fine."

"Someone else?"

"Like someone who is more flamboyant or nonbinary. My friend Morgan likes to wear eyeliner on days when they're feeling femme. Or on days when they're feeling masc." His expression turned thoughtful. "Actually Morgan wears eyeliner pretty much all the time. And that's fine. Just like Peyton has no interest in it. And not because she's bi or anything. She gets eye infections every time she goes near eye makeup. Even if the shit's brand new."

"Right." I was getting confused. "So you're in love with a football player."

Another sigh. "Love's complicated."

"Undoubtedly."

"I mean, I barely know the guy."

"The one you met the first day of school?"

"Yes."

"You appeared quite taken with him even then. I assume things haven't gotten better?"

"Watching him wear that football uniform? With the tightest ass you've ever—"

I squeaked. An actual swear-to-God squeak.

"What?"

"Thinking about…football players'…uh…tight ends…"

"They're called asses. Or butts. And this guy's got a glorious one. All nice and tight and—"

I squeaked.

Holden snickered. "Seriously? You're in high school, and the words I'm using to describe a guy's ass are setting you off? Man, it's the twenty-first century." He pointed to the history books. "They were uptight. We"—he waved between the two of us—"don't have to be."

"I was…" *Hmm*. "I was raised in a different time."

He frowned. "What the hell does that mean? A *different time*? Like you come to school earlier than me?" He scratched his nose. "You're weird."

"Well…" I drew in a deep breath. "I might've met someone as well." I wasn't going to address his query about my *different time* comment. Why he could see me was beyond me. I wanted to cultivate this relationship to see if I could get to the bottom of this anomaly.

"Yeah?" Holden perked up. "Who? Wait, weren't you in love with a football player?"

I cleared my throat. "I'm not certain. He's…moved on with his life." *Or so I assume. We haven't seen each other in an incredibly long time.*

"Did you ever tell him that you loved him?"

"No. Absolutely not."

"Do you wish you'd told him?"

That question had me pausing. Did I wish I'd told Frank how I felt? What would life have looked like for me—for us—if I had shared my truth? We wouldn't have wound up together. Or…I hesitated. Gay people did that. Got together. Got married. Lived happy lives together. That was a thing these days. Hadn't been back then. That being said, I'd known a couple of *roommates* who'd most likely been more than that. Pinedale was pretty good about *live and let live*. As long as the *living* wasn't shoved in other people's faces.

Right?

"I'm going to take that as a *no*."

"That would be correct."

"Regrets?" He continued to tap his pen on his textbook.

Although the sound irritated me, I could tolerate a

fair amount of annoyance. All manner of weird things took place in these stacks. Still, I considered his question. "We wouldn't have worked out. Regardless, I wish I'd been more true to myself."

"I'd say that sounds like regrets." He squinted, as if trying to see me better. As if trying to see through me. As if trying to see inside my soul. "You're young…" He blinked. "Holy shit—I don't even know your name. Did I introduce myself?"

"You're Holden."

"Right." He frowned, then rolled his hand as if to indicate my turn to speak had arrived.

"Willie."

He laughed. I held his gaze as his laughter died.

"Oh, damn. That's rough, man. Is that short for something? William or something?"

"My father's name was William. My birth certificate says *William Arnold* as well."

"Is Arnold a middle or last name?"

I winced. "Middle."

Another laugh burst out of him. "So your dad is William."

"And my uncle is Arnold."

"So you had the choice between Willie and Arnie?"

I rolled my eyes. "Yes, that about sums it up. Willie just…seemed easier."

"Was Bill ever a possibility?"

"Uncle on my mother's side. And don't suggest Billy—that was my cousin. In my time, lots of boys were named after their fathers. I was actually William the fourth."

"That's a lot of pressure to put on a kid. Because, like, if you don't have a kid, then you're, like, breaking the line of lineage." He stopped the infernal pen tapping. "I got that right, right?"

"Yes."

He tapped the pen.

I shot out my hand to stop him. Of course, my hand went right through the book on the shelf between us.

Holden leapt up, backed away, and nearly knocked the study carrel next to him over.

"Oh dear."

"Oh dear? Are you fucking kidding me? You shit." He hissed the word.

I shrugged. Then, finding courage, I walked around the stacks to his spot.

He shot furtive glances in all directions.

"No one can see me."

"Okay, first, you can't say that. *I* can see you. Second, I'm now talking to a…what? Ghost? Spirit? Apparition? Do you even know what the hell you are?"

"I go with ghost. I'm one of a large number in the school and surrounding grounds. I'm thinking there's some kind of ley line—"

"A what now?"

"Ley line." I tried to figure out the best way to explain them. Truthfully, I'd been a ghost for thirty-five years, and I didn't understand them. Mary had tried to explain them, but I hadn't understood her. But then, she'd been around here a lot longer than me. And she'd known some real—like, really real—witches in her time. I waved him off. "Never mind."

Again, he gazed around, even ducking behind the stacks, then coming back. After a moment, he grinned. "Okay, nice au naturel look."

I stood a little taller. "What's wrong with it?"

65

He smothered a laugh. "Uh, nothing." He arched his eyebrow. "You ever try a towel or something?"

I suspected my cheeks were pinkening. Wait…did ghosts blush? Since I couldn't see myself in a mirror, I had no idea. "I tried that. I was reaching for a towel when, you know…" I whispered harshly. "But…I have scrawny chicken legs, and I didn't want to, you know, have Frank, uh, the other boys, see them."

"You'll have to tell me more about this Frank. Why are you naked?"

"I was in the locker room."

He snickered. "You perv on naked boys? That's…" He appeared to think about it. "Yeah, if I was dead and had nothing else to do, I might look at naked teenagers all day."

"I meant the day I died."

"When was that?"

"Thirty-five years ago."

"Oh."

I nodded.

"And you were, what, seventeen?"

I nodded.

"So you're, like…" He gazed upward.

"Fifty-two," I supplied.

"Okay, well, that is pervy."

"I'm really seventeen." I snuck a peek down at my body, which still hadn't hit full puberty. *A late bloomer* as my mother liked to say. Barely over five feet, no appreciable chest hair, acne… I felt the compulsion to defend myself. "I'm seventeen, Holden. I didn't get to grow up. To go to college. To find someone to love. It's just me, the teachers, the students who never stay, and the ghosts who never leave."

He squinted. "Exactly how many ghosts are there?"

I waved him off.

"Well, okay then." He didn't appear offended as he moved closer. "Now, you think you might've derailed me, but I've got an excellent memory. Especially for gossip. So tell me—you said you met someone? Another ghost?"

After a long moment, I cleared my throat. "He's older than me."

"Like, by how much?"

"Oh, like a hundred and forty-five years."

He plopped back down on his chair. "Okay, you *have* to tell me everything."

And I was about to when three teenagers rounded the corner.

Holden glanced from me to them and then back again. He managed a smile as he rose. "Hey, Eric, Kayla, and Aubrey. How are you?"

The guy cocked his head. "We heard you talking to someone?"

"You could hear the guy?" Holden blinked.

One of the young women, on the petite side with a black-colored bob haircut, shook her head. "Nah, we heard *you* talking."

"Yeah." The second girl nodded. "And I told Aubrey you were just talking to yourself, but she swore you were having a conversation."

Okay, the first girl was Aubrey, so the willowy strawberry-blonde must be Kayla. Obviously, the fit guy who towered over Holden was Eric. I guessed he participated in some kind of sports, but I didn't always get it right.

"No one else here." Holden cut me a furtive glance.

I could've hidden, but frankly, I was curious whether the three could see me.

Clearly not.

I couldn't figure out if I was disappointed or still intrigued only Holden could see me. Why him? Why after all this time? Because he was gay and out? He wasn't the first kid to be so in this library, and he wouldn't be the last.

"We were wondering if you and Peyton wanted to come to a party on Saturday night." Aubrey grinned. "You don't work Saturdays, right?"

Holden shook his head.

"So you have to come." Eric smiled. "We're having a games night. I know it sounds boring—"

"It sounds perfect." Holden returned Eric's smile.

"Larry, Gary, and Dominic aren't invited." Kayla made a face. "Like, that move the first day of classes was so lame."

Was this the incident that had upset Holden two weeks ago?

"We're inclusive." Kayla grinned. "And I think Eric can kick the butt of anyone who doesn't agree with that."

"I'd prefer no violence." Holden managed a smile, but I caught the strain.

Aubrey gently nudged him. "We think it's cool you and Peyton came out. And the other kids too. If you can do that, we can stand by you. We've invited some other people as well."

Holden did a weird shrug thing. I didn't understand it until he followed up with, "Any football players? Cheerleaders?"

Eric nodded enthusiastically. "Yeah. It's going to be a great crowd."

After a moment, Holden glanced my way. Then he turned back to the three. "Count us in."

Kayla did a little excited dance.

I might've as well. For Holden. And the fact he had allies in the school.

Chapter Seven

Peyton

Mondays suck.

Last week of September. Third Monday of the school year. A night off of practice. A night my stupid bestie stocked shelves at the grocery store. A night to myself.

Which I pretty much hated. Before the whole Susan thing, I would've been surrounded by a dozen other girls. Some popular and some not so. Just…people liked to hang out with me. Or they had. Now some people worried I had cooties.

Well, maybe that was an exaggeration. I didn't get invitations from people I'd considered friends. They were *too busy* or *not today*. Castra flat out said her mother forbade it. The mother on her fourth marriage. Divorce was okay. Being a dyke wasn't. And hell, I didn't even fully identify as a lesbian. I was bi. Getting that across to people was challenging.

Are you sure you don't prefer guys?
Are you sure you don't prefer girls?
Do you want everyone to yourself?
Are you just indecisive?

That one amused me. I could be very decisive. If I saw someone I was attracted to and they were single, I'd see if they might be interested. Some people were attractive on the outside and rotten in their soul. Other people might be ordinary looking—by society's shallow standards—but have hearts of gold. *Those* were the people I tried to spend time with. Like Holden. He was nice-looking. More importantly, he was the sweetest guy I knew. Good thing I wasn't attracted to him. I didn't believe someone could change their orientation, but I'd platonically marry him if he asked me. If that was our best shot. If neither of us found someone better. Better than some of the other people in town.

Platonically marry? What does that even mean? You'll get out of this place. You'll meet someone. Right. College felt a million years away instead of just one—

"Peyton!" A voice rang out.

I spun to find the object of my desire running toward me, waving her hand. *Oh God, why does she have to be so gorgeous? And that's not what's most important.* I might've first noticed Juliette for her looks, but her sweet nature kept me hanging around, even knowing we could only ever be friends. Somehow, in three years, we'd only been in a handful of classes together. We were friendly, but we weren't friends. I'd never expected her to say my name in that bubbly, cheerful way.

"Uh, hey." I managed a little wave.

She planted herself before me and offered the widest smile with such perfect teeth. *She must've had braces—no one has teeth that perfect.* Then I remembered Larry's were just that perfect. *Hope they get knocked out when he plays...basketball? Hey, it could happen. Elbow to the face... Focus.*

"Hi." Her smile might've turned a little rueful. "We haven't really talked—which is weird, but whatever. Anyway, I wanted to say thanks for that first day when you threw down in the guys' faces—especially Dominic's. He's an, um, well, not a nice person."

Asshole? Shithead? Life must be tough when she felt she couldn't swear.

"And it makes me feel glad that there's someone around who will defend me if I'm ever in trouble—"

My brain skipped right from cursing to protection. "What the actual fuck? *In trouble?* Has he been bothering you as you walk home from school?" *Well, duh, he's one of the bullies. Even cheer squad captains get harassed.*

"Well, maybe…" She grabbed a strand of her hair and twirled it in her long, elegant fingers. That gorgeous, bouncy, curly hair. No cheer practice today meant she could let her hair do what it was meant to do—those perfect tight curls I adored. Mentally, I shook my head. "Screw him. I'll walk with you."

Juliette blinked. "But you live over on Waltham Street. My house is way over on Graves Drive. We're in opposite directions."

"Doesn't matter." I meant it. Juliette might be taller and have better muscles, but I was scrappy. Having an older sister on the wrestling team had taught me plenty about self-preservation. Had taught me a few dirty moves as well—but I wasn't supposed to share that with anyone. "I'll still walk with you. They can all go to hell."

She blinked…possibly at my vehemence.

"Well, we both have calculus with Mrs. Bletchley. Maybe we could, um, make the walk worthwhile. Do you have an assignment due tomorrow?"

"As it happens…I do." My calculus textbook, though, was at home. While I struggled with biology, calculus came easy. "Do you need help?"

"I…could use a hand. If you don't mind." She blinked rapidly.

She's not fluttering her lashes. Although that would be cute. "Do you have something in your eye? Do you need eyedrops? Or is it an eyelash? I had one in my eye the other day, and they're a bitch—"

"I'm fine, Peyton. Just, you know, the sun."

We were in the shade of a tree, but maybe the sun was shining through at an odd angle? "Right, you ready to go?"

"Yes."

"Oh, my textbook is at my house. I mean, we can share…" Because sharing sounded amazing.

"Great, let's go to your house."

I blinked. My little bungalow versus her near-mansion-sized house?

Maybe she doesn't want me to meet her parents. My parents wouldn't be home for a couple of hours, and they were going out for their anniversary dinner tonight. Mom had been embarrassed when she suggested this was a romantic meal between just the two of them.

Well, duh. Like I want to see that shmoopiness. Twenty-five years and going strong. Right. Because *that's* what mattered.

She gestured. "So let's walk to your house, pick up your assignment, then you can come and study at my house. My dad gets back at six. He'll drop you home."

"Uh, great." *Okay, so meeting her parents is okay.* God knew mine wouldn't have an issue. I waited, but she didn't do anything but grin.

After a long moment, we headed off.

To my house.

Alone.

Calm down.

Wait…how does she know I live on Waltham Street? Huh…maybe she knows where Holden lives. They…talk more than I do. Damn. Should've queried him more.

We turned onto the first street in our brief journey when she gestured. "Mrs. Bletchley's pretty brutal."

"I had her in tenth grade. I passed"—*second highest grade*—"but tough. It's biology that's going to be my downfall."

"I can help you with that. I aced biology. Which is great for my chances of getting early admittance into an excellent school. Anything that gets me closer to med school." She sighed. "I plan to go to Howard University for my undergrad and then either Harvard or Stanford for medical school."

Something in her tone had me taking notice. "Howard's a great school. And Harvard? Wow."

"You know Charlie's a shoo-in for law school there." Pride radiated from her.

Charlie was her older brother. *Wasn't he valedictorian? Will Juliette be ours?*

"Of course." I didn't say her parents must be loaded to have two kids heading to Harvard for med and law school. Maybe scholarships? But she'd have to be perfect for that. Juliette was smart, no question about it, but I hadn't heard of her excelling in academics. Not top-of-her-class smart, anyway. I needed to pay closer attention. "Wow. Harvard."

"What about you? If you're good at calculus, that must mean you're planning to do some STEM program, right?"

We turned onto the next street. The houses were getting a little smaller. Some might be a little shabbier.

Not our house. We might not be rich, but my parents kept a meticulous lawn. I'd once asked why we didn't live in a richer neighborhood. My mom had pointed out our house was paid for and they were setting aside money for my education. And although Lily had landed an amazing scholarship, she needed help too.

I'd been embarrassed I'd asked and had taken pride in our home after that.

Shit. I haven't answered her question. "I was thinking UNC. Chapel Hill's close by, right? Or NCSU. Raleigh's not that far, and they've got a good program. Or Duke, of course."

"Staying in North Carolina is…a choice."

"Yeah. You'll still be close to home. I mean, DC's not so far. Not like Massachusetts or California."

"Howard's an excellent school."

"No question."

"My mom went to Howard."

"Ah. Well, my parents…" I swallowed. "Dad went to a college farther south of here." *Like, way south.* "He got a job up here, and they moved. Mom finished high school and worked to pay for Dad's school. She would've gone herself—that was the plan. But she got pregnant with Lily, and you know how it goes." We turned onto Waltham Street. *Be proud. You have a great family. Quirky, but great.* "Uh, this house."

"Oh, Peyton, it's so pretty."

The red brick with bright-white trim that Dad had painted over the summer was cute, I supposed. With mom's meticulous gardening, this was a welcoming home. "Yeah, let me just get my—" The front door swung open. Apparently, Mom was home after all. Something must've happened with her reservation.

Mom stepped out. "Come in, honey. Your dad got hung up at work, but he should be home soon. I was able to move our reservation, so you don't need to worry—we'll be out of here soon." She waved us in.

I indicated Juliette should go first. Then winced because I just didn't know how this would go. "Mom, this is Juliette." I figured my mom could introduce herself.

"Oh, hello." Mom closed the door and ushered Juliette into the living room. "You're so pretty. I love your nails."

We all looked at Juliette's trimmed but painted nails.

"Where do you get them done? I would love for Peyton to be into nails and makeup and all that, but she's not." Before I could get a word in edgewise, she pointed to Juliette. "Oh, hun, I love your bag. Where did you get it?"

Juliette blinked. "At a store in New York. My parents took me there when we were visiting my brother in Cambridge."

Mom blinked. "Oh. Right. Oh. Harvard?"

"Yes." Juliette offered her megawatt smile. "That's my brother."

"You know my daughter Lily's at the University of South Carolina?" She didn't wait for an answer. "Studying aerospace engineering."

Juliette glanced over at me. "No, I hadn't realized. She's a few years older than us, right?"

Mom waved. "Of course. Yes, she's five years older than Peyton." She grinned. "I'm proud of both my girls. Did Peyton tell you her score on her latest test in calculus?"

"Oh God, Mom, please—"

"Top score. Of all the classes."

Juliette glanced over at me. "Oh, really?"

"And she's done all her assignments for the next month. Early."

"Oh, really? And here I thought we'd be doing the assignment together."

I winced. "Uh…I was going to consult my notes." *Goddamn it, Mom*. I couldn't blame her. She had a daughter in a prestigious engineering program and another daughter who excelled at calculus…but sucked at biology.

"We think Peyton's going to follow in her sister's footsteps."

"They're big shoes to fill, Mom." *And not what I want.*

Juliette gazed at me as if I'd spoken the words aloud, a little knowing smile on her lips.

"Please stop." I had to somehow fix this out-of-control train. Better to go back to the tried and true. "I know I'm a total disappointment to you in the daughter department. Not painting my nails and all. But could you *not* treat my friends like this?"

Mom met my stare.

For a moment, I thought I might've hurt her feelings.

"You are *not* a disappointment. I would love to see you wear…a blouse or two? Look at Juliette's skirt."

Nope, didn't hurt her feelings at all. I'd noticed Juliette's skirt. Not too short, but still showing off miles of beautiful legs. As opposed to my rather boring ones I kept hidden beneath my jeans.

"I'm not going to wear a skirt, Mom."

"But you'd look so pretty."

Juliette tilted her head. "I think she looks great in

jeans. I mean, if you're comfortable—"

"I have to get my assignment." With my cheeks burning a brutal fire, I beat a path to my room. As much as I wanted to shut the door, hide under the covers, and never come out again, I couldn't help but listen at the door. I couldn't hear the words being exchanged, though, so I grabbed my calculus assignment and made my way back to the living room.

Juliette had dropped her bag and toed off her cute shoes.

"I thought we were going back to your place." I didn't phrase that as a question.

After a moment, she put her shoes back on, hefted her backpack, and waved to my mom. "Nice to meet you, Mrs. Morris."

"Oh, lovely to meet you, dear."

I winced. And was almost to the door when my mom grabbed my arm and pulled me aside.

"I like her. Feel free to bring her back anytime."

Somehow, I didn't die of embarrassment.

A close call…but I managed.

Chapter Eight

Duncan

I waved to Mary, Fiona, and Aaron—one of the newer ghosts—as I continued my search for Willie. We hadn't spoken for a few weeks. We'd never been close, but he'd been acting extra weird recently, and I wanted to know why. More than that, loneliness had crept into my bones again.

Unsurprisingly, I discovered Willie in the locker room.

Alone.

His place of refuge. Well, there and the library. "How are you doing?" I sat on the bench next to him. "I had to search to find you."

"Go away, Duncan. I'm…meditating."

One of those newfangled things I'd seen people doing. Sitting, closing their eyes, breathing—okay, that confused me because didn't everyone except ghosts breathe?—and…clearing their minds. I sometimes drifted away from the school building itself and as far as the lake, which bordered the school grounds. I couldn't go beyond that, though. And anyway, the meditation instructors always struck me as kooky. Not as out there as some of the stuff that went down in the sixties, but definitely not anything we'd ever have contemplated in my day.

"Come on," I urged Willie. "I'm bored. It's night, and school's closed. Neither of us needs sleep. So talk to me."

"I don't have any clothes on."

He never wore clothes. The unfortunate situation of having died while naked. Sometimes, when he spotted me, he looked embarrassed. Truly, I didn't understand him. But I wanted to. Of all the ghosts around here, he intrigued me the most these days. He was one of the younger ones. Thirty-five years was damn young around here.

Well, Aaron was even newer, but I wanted him to settle in before I approached him. Being dead could disconcert a person.

"I know you're not wearing clothes." *Highly aware.* "I don't care. Come talk to me. There's only nutty, old Mrs. Bletchley and Coach Pinker among the flesh-and-bloods. I'm not in the mood for math lessons nor looking at football plays. Honestly, how is all that complicated stuff involved? You throw the ball. Hopefully, someone on your team catches it. Why all those *plays* are involved, I'll never understand." I sighed. "So save me from them."

He blinked up at me behind his glasses. They were so thick they made him look owlish. Unfortunate that dying hadn't fixed his poor eyesight.

"You think they're just *plays*?" He said the word with incredulity. "They're critical. Coach needs to be able to call a play so the players know…how to, like…" He pulled his lower lip through his teeth. "Well, you know."

"No, I don't know. We didn't have football in my day. And when they first started playing it, so many years ago, it looked very different. Today there's all this"—I motioned up and down my body—"equipment."

"And those tight pants." Willie sighed.

My interest piqued, I eyed him. "Yes, the pants are definitely tight. They weren't always that way. Well, back in the forties, their pants were different."

"I've never seen photos. Didn't the school burn down, like, seventy-two years ago?"

Slowly, I nodded. "Yes."

"Were you in it?"

"One of my nights walking the perimeter of the property."

"You do that a lot."

"This is not a place I wish to remain a prisoner within." And since I didn't want to go down this particular train of thought, I offered a tight smile. "The fire was tragic. But only one death."

"Right. I grew up hearing the stories. My grandparents went to the school before the fire. They told me the story." I glanced out toward the trees. "I hadn't noticed you walking the perimeter. That…feels very sad. But you weren't a student, obviously."

"No." I gazed at my uniform. "Obviously."

"But did you die on school grounds? I haven't found a ghost that didn't. Admittedly, I don't talk to all of them. Some kind of creep me out, you know?"

"Uh, certainly." They didn't creep me out. I was so bored that any interaction with any spirit interested me. But not all were friendly. And since I didn't share any of my past, some might not find me personable either. "Yes, I died on school grounds. Unpleasantly."

He pointed to my uniform. "You look pretty good."

I straightened. "For reasons I do not understand, I

was returned to my state just before…my death. Perhaps because I would give people nightmares if they saw me as I'd been when I died."

Willie sighed. "How come the *powers that be* weren't that kind to me?" He indicated his nakedness.

Personally, I found him adorable. All porcelain-white skin, light-blond hair, light-blue eyes, and, well, the cutest dick. Not that I was looking, of course. Because that would be rude.

Occasionally, though, from a distance, I either spotted his tight ass or his pretty dick. I was only human. If we had a naked female ghost walking around, I might take a quick peek too. I hadn't seen a naked woman in over one hundred and fifty years. Because, obviously, I didn't hang out in the girls' showers. And that one time I'd found Bart and Clarice having sex—was that seventy-one or seventy-two? Anyway, I'd backed away. Usually, I could spot when a couple was about to have carnal relations, and I'd make myself scarce. Seriously, who knew so much groping, French kissing, and outright sex would occur on school grounds?

I blinked. "So how did you die?"

"You don't know?"

I shook my head. "No, I don't. I wasn't wherever you were when it happened. You were in shock for about a dozen years. After that, when you appeared ready to talk about it, I seemed to freak you out. After another dozen years, it felt rude."

He offered me a small smile. "But now another almost dozen years have passed, and you think it might be time?"

I returned his smile. "Certainly."

He sighed. "It's such a stupid story. I was in the

shower, and…" He winced. "I slipped, cracked my head open on the sharp edge, and I died. One-in-a-million shot, the coroner said."

"Interesting. I must've been elsewhere, because I didn't see a coroner. Just the ambulance. The vehicle arrived with sirens blaring and left without them." Even I'd understood, although we hadn't had ambulances in my day, that either something good happened—the person wasn't urgent—or something bad happened, and they'd died. I was surprised how many people had died here over the years.

"You're not the oldest ghost."

I frowned.

"Well, like, Fiona's been here longer than you. And Mary's older than you. You're just a couple of years older than me when you died."

Don't remind me. A mere three years. But even those brought a lot of emotional maturity. Not to mention over one hundred years of dead experiences, if I chose to mark time that way.

Which I did. Made it easier to keep a distance.

If you wanted distance, why did you seek him out?

Oh, be quiet. Having long periods of time when I only had myself as company—because sometimes I wanted to be alone—I often had extensive conversations with myself about my life, my choices, and how I'd wound up in this exact spot in North Carolina. All of which tended to drag me down to, as the modern counselors said, a dark place.

But hearing about how a seventeen-year-old cracked his head open and died seemed…more distant? Less personal?

"Hello, Duncan." Willie waved his hand in front of

my face. "Are you in there? You spend a lot of time thinking. Doesn't that hurt?"

I chuckled. "Perhaps." I gazed at him again. "You know, if you were alive, I'd offer you my coat so you wouldn't be cold."

"But I'm not cold. Wouldn't it great to be cold again?"

"I remember being cold. Our winter campaign as we moved south from Boston toward Virginia was brutal. Some nights we nearly froze to death." I considered. "Then, conversely, we'd been so hot that final summer this far south."

"What was it like to fight?"

After a long moment of debate, I let myself slide back into the memory. "Detestable. Smelly. Soul-crushing." I drew in a breath, even though I no longer consumed oxygen—more in remembrance of what a deep breath felt like. "America is an amazing country. Despite my birth into slavery, once I was a free man and had time to read, I'd always found the promise of the constitution to be my lodestar."

"Lodestar? Are you a sailor?"

Amused, I shook my head. "No, but I knew a couple who joined the army. Anyway"—I was *not* going to be distracted—"eventually, when I discovered that not only had the South lost the war but also that slaves were free, I…" I'd laughed like a madman and then cried, though my ghost tears were dry. Cursed and danced on the imagined graves of my enemies, and cried again for all the friends I'd lost. I would not burden this young man with those details. "I rejoiced."

"As you should. You helped secure that victory." His eyes shone luminous in the overly bright fluorescent lights.

Everything felt so bright. Like sunlight brought inside. I had been accustomed to candlelight, and looking back made the familiar modernity seem strange again. Nothing like that ambiance in this school, that was for certain.

I cleared my throat. "Yes, well, things weren't simple back then, were they? We had theoretical freedom for a while. Congress even passed legislation. But I'm certain you've heard of Jim Crow."

Slowly, he nodded.

"Things went backward." So I'd heard and read, trapped here in the school, watching only White students come in the door, year after year. "Or perhaps they'd never really moved forward. Black folk were free, but plenty of oppression still existed."

Willie winced.

"Things changed in the sixties and seventies. For the better." I scratched my chin, which always itched even though that wasn't possible—the memory of an itchy beard, perhaps. "Then things didn't look so bad. America even had a Black president."

"Yeah, that was pretty cool. I wish I could've voted for him."

"Yes, me too." I contemplated my next words. "Things haven't steadily improved. And I'm not going to wax on about it. You can attend a history class, or a politics class, to get a fuller picture." I didn't want to bring down the conversation. Although I could tell plenty of positive stories as well. Which was why I loved my country, despite her flaws.

Willie sighed. "Will we always be ghosts?"

His question startled me. "Well, given it's been one

hundred and sixty years for me, I'm thinking this is a permanent state. And Mary's been here far longer. Fiona a bit less time, but still longer than me. Why?"

He pulled his lower lip through his teeth. "I just wondered what might happen if, you know, two ghosts fall in love."

Intrigued, I made myself more comfortable—as if that was a thing. "Tell me more."

"Oh, I think I hear Mary. I gotta go."

Before I could react, he was through the wall and gone. The familiar whistling sound followed him.

Strange young man.

Wanting a breath of fresh air—which was more of an echo of a memory than a reality—and missing my patrol of the grounds, I headed out into the early fall crisp air. Regretting as always that I'd miss the smell of autumn. Odd that I could hear and see while not being able to touch or smell. And here in the mountains, the leaves would be soon changing their colors. My favorite time of year.

And thus, the Earth would continue spinning, and I would continue walking alone.

Well, mostly.

Chapter Nine

Holden

When Oliver landed a job stocking shelves with me at the grocery store, I'd thought I'd died and gone to Heaven. Now, after three weeks, I'd say Hell was a more apt description. We worked the same shifts because, naturally, our practices tended to fall on the same nights. Mr. O was the best boss ever. He let me work whenever my band schedule allowed. Once or twice, when Isabella was younger, I'd needed to bring her with me. Mr. O had offered me the night off to watch my sister, but I'd needed the money. So Izzy had sat in the company lunchroom with her coloring book while I worked—checking on her frequently. The other store staff had done the same. For a nine-year-old, she'd been such a great kid. I was relieved I could leave her at home alone now when both Mom and I worked.

Oliver placed the last box of cereal in the slot, precisely centered the row, and grinned.

"Perfect." Saying the word felt lame. Because, of course, everything Oliver did was perfect. Hell, *he* was perfect. And such a great guy. *And completely out of bounds. Ha! A football reference.* I considered. Untouchable? Definitely straight and since I didn't try to turn guys—no matter how gorgeous, sweet, and…perfect—I wouldn't go there. A small voice in my brain kept reminding me that I didn't *know* he was straight. *Plenty of gay people in the proverbial closet.*

I finished my row. "We need to move to produce."

We broke down the boxes and headed to the back to put them in the recycle bin.

Plenty of suddenly-turning-gay stories out there. Probably more in fiction than in real life. How many people went along in their straight lives, met someone of the same sex, blinked, and suddenly became bi or gay? *Not many…I don't think.* Truthfully, I didn't have a lot of experience, and I basically never left Pinedale. Plenty of gay clubs in Raleigh. And I intended to take full advantage. I just needed to turn twenty-one and to find the courage. Peyton would come with me, especially if we found a broadly queer venue. If we both wound up in Raleigh for school. Or maybe when we came home for summer holidays.

Mr. O was making noises about me committing to working here every summer until I graduated college.

As much as I wanted to get out and see the world, Isabella still needed me. Maybe not to babysit her every night, but I was a good influence.

Or at least I tried to be.

We tossed the cardboard into a bin at the back of the store, reentered the storage area, and then Oliver pointed to the fridge.

I nodded.

He pushed the trolley while I held the door open.

Together, we loaded the smaller-quantity fruits and vegetables. Then we loaded crates of apples, pears, and oranges onto the dolly. He stacked one more than I would've if I'd been the one pulling it. Because, right, *muscles.*

We made our way to the produce section, and I started with the leafy vegetables while he tackled the apples.

"You remember you have to rotate the stock, right?" I glanced over.

He rolled his gorgeous deep-blue eyes. "Yeah, I remember." His red hair appeared more coppery in the crappy store lighting. *What would it look like in the gym locker room light? If I happened upon him when he was changing…*

Knock it off.

"Did you say something?" Oliver leaned so he was within my line of sight.

Damn, did I say that out loud? "Uh, me? No, nothing." I might've squeaked that. Much like Willie when my teasing went too far with him. For a teenager, he was a bit of a prude. We hung out whenever I had a spare block. At the back corner with the European history books. We'd yet to be disturbed. "That was Ms. Cracken with the shopping cart. Did you see her? Do you have her for any classes?"

He didn't. I had his entire schedule memorized—teachers and all.

I kept right on going. "She's a great English teacher. Way younger than Mrs. Bletchley. I mean, Mom says I'm not allowed to talk shit about older people—"

"You're not—"

"—but she's ancient. I feel like maybe a younger math teacher would be better."

"Juliette would agree." Oliver reached to the back of the bin to secure the fresh apples.

Oh sweet baby Jesus…that ass… I blinked. "Uh, Juliette?"

Oliver gave me a funny look. "Yeah, I told you that she's struggling with calculus. Peyton's tutoring her. And in turn, Juliette's helping Peyton with biology."

I snickered. "Yeah, Pey would need help with that."

He cocked his head. "You didn't know? I thought Peyton told you everything." He put an odd emphasis on *everything*.

Damn. *Did she? Did I forget? Am I being a terrible friend again?* Pey and I regularly took swipes at each other for not paying enough attention about the other's drama because we had so much of our own. "I want to say she does, but…" I shrugged as I removed the wilted lettuce. Not too bad. Mr. O would run it to the vet clinic where the rescue rabbits would demolish it in less than a day. I always wanted to bring a rabbit home, but Mom was adamant she didn't need another mouth to feed.

And she was right.

I changed the subject. "Any badly bruised apples? Mrs. McPhee's dog loves those."

Oliver held up two golden delicious with brown spots. Yeah, I could cut around those for Rupert. The Pekinese might even let me pet him if I brought enough treats. He was…particular. Adored Peyton, of course, when she came with me to visit. When I went alone, the little shit barely gave me the time of day. "Great. Want to put them on my cart? Next to the lettuce?"

"Sure." He resumed his work. "Uncle Jeremiah's been asking questions about me working."

"He doesn't like you doing it? You're still getting your schoolwork done, right? That was the deal?" I moved to the peppers and started sorting them by color.

"Yeah. He just…he's got a good job. Aunt Leslie's got a good job."

"Well, you're not taking this one away from someone who needs it." I tossed that nugget in just in case that was the issue.

He shook his head. "Nah. Just…they're worried about school, and—" He sniffed.

Oh, he was working near the onions. The skin should've protected him from the smell, though. "And," I prompted.

"They don't really get it." He moved on to the oranges. "I need to feel like I'm contributing. I've brought nothing to help them out."

I cocked my head. I understood wanting to contribute. I had this job to help Mom. But if I had more time to study, I might have better prospects for college. "Why would you need to bring something to help out, Oliver? You're the kid, and they're the adults. If they didn't want you, I'm sure they could've foisted you off on someone else." The foster system was full of kids who didn't have someone. "You miss your parents, don't you?"

He met my gaze and blinked several times. "Yeah. Sometimes I think it might've been okay if I'd had a sibling—someone to share the grief. But I had my grandma, and…we had each other."

"And now you don't have her."

"Well, she's not dead. Just…" He glanced back at the oranges. "She's got Alzheimer's. So…it's almost like she is dead. She doesn't recognize me anymore. And she's frail."

I stopped sorting peppers and made my way over to him. "That's rough. I mean, losing a parent is bad enough—I went through that. But losing two? Then the grandmother who's taken care of you?" I wanted to say

I wasn't certain how I'd cope, but those didn't feel like the right words. Nothing felt right. "Do you…want a hug?" The store was pretty empty this late on a Sunday night, but Ms. Cracken was around and maybe a few of our friends.

Still, when he nodded, I opened my arms. In the end, given our height difference, I wound up resting my head tucked under his chin with my arms around his torso, holding him tight.

After what felt like forever but was only about a minute, a person clearing their throat had us pulling away.

Being the brave one—or so I told myself—I faced the interloper.

Ms. Cracken.

I smiled. "How can I help you?"

She pointed to the asparagus on my cart. "That's fresher, isn't it?"

"How many would you like?" I kept my smile plastered on. *How's Oliver doing? He's still behind me, but I don't want to look…*

"Twenty-five. I'm having a dinner party on Friday night for eight. Three bundles will work. And I'm making a cheese sauce to go on it."

I nearly winced at *asparagus*, but I perked up at *cheese sauce*. Cheese made everything better. *Everything.* "Sounds delicious."

She offered me a benevolent smile. "Yes, I believe so." She leaned in. "Is Mr. Barton okay? Is there something I can do to help?"

Ms. Cracken was old-fashioned South, and she insisted we use each other's last names.

I cleared my throat. "Mr. Barton is fine. Just…" I

floundered.

"Ah, I understand."

As I gazed into her hazel eyes, I believed her. "I'll take care of him."

She appeared like she was going to pat my hand or something but pulled back at the last moment. "See that you do." Louder, she said, "Looking forward to seeing Friday's game, Mr. Barton."

"Me too, Ms. Cracken." Oliver gave her a huge smile. "Thanks so much. Coach Pinker's great."

That might've been a little over-the-top, but we'd won our division two years ago, so that meant something.

Ms. Cracken met my gaze. "Try to have fun. You worry too much."

Before I could respond, she wheeled her cart out of our section and headed toward the cashiers.

"She's, uh, nice." Oliver continued to sort the oranges.

"Nosy, you mean." Still, despite my words, I had a smile.

"What do you have to worry about?" He cut me a look.

Working with him for weeks meant he knew about my home situation. "Just…she knows about my mom's work hours. Which means she knows about me. Despite that, I hope she winds up being Isabella's teacher when she gets to Pinedale High."

"You're a little protective of your sister, huh?"

"Yep." I popped the P. "She's a good kid."

"You're her brother—of course she would be."

I rolled my eyes. "Plenty of siblings in no way resemble each other. Dominic's older sister is a sweetheart, and he's a shit. He hasn't given you a hard time again, has he?"

Oliver pretended to dust his shirt. "I kicked the winning field goal in my first game. No one gives me a hard time." Then his face fell a little—taking a darker quality.

"What?"

"I'm just thinking about the nasty things people do say."

My hackles rose. "About who?"

"Oh." He winced. "Uh…never mind?"

"Oliver." I started working on the asparagus so Mr. O got his money's worth while paying me a generous salary. Still, I glanced at my—

Huh. Friend? Coworker? Dude I wished I could date?

He waved me off as he finished with the oranges and moved on to the pears. "Does Mrs. McPhee's dog like pears?"

"Rupert the Precious? He eats anything, and yes, pears don't give him indigestion. Thanks for thinking of him—that was kind."

"There's only one pear."

"That's okay. I don't want to give the little shit, uh, twit, too many treats."

Oliver chuckled, but I barely heard him.

We worked along until we finished with produce. "We have noodles and dog food left. We could split up…" *Please say no. Please say no*.

"I think we work faster when we work together. I can put the bags of dog food on the dolly while you pile the noodle boxes on your cart. Not sure that's the most efficient—"

"It works. Things are so much faster with you than alone." I got more done, which meant Mr. O had less he had to do himself. He filled in and picked up the slack whenever something didn't get finished. I felt guilty if I didn't get everything perfect, but sometimes I had to quit after having done my best.

Working efficiently, we found ourselves in the dog food section. I tried to haul the twenty-five-pound bags off the shelf, but Oliver gently nudged me out of the way. I organized the cans while he added the newer bags on the bottom and then put the older ones on top. He dusted off his hands in evident pleasure at finishing the task.

Applauding at how quick he works would be cheesy…right?

Yeah, probably.

We scooted over to the noodle aisle. I used my pocket knife to open the cases while he moved the few remaining containers to the cart.

He cleared his throat.

Does he have allergies or something? He seemed to be clearing his throat a lot tonight. Or…well, more than usual?

I met his gaze. "Yeah?"

"So what's it like being gay?"

My knife slipped, and I damn near cut through the boxes of pasta inside the big box. "Shit."

He held out his hands. "Sorry. Sorry. I'm so sorry."

"Yeah, I got it." I reoriented myself and started again. "You want to know what it's like to be gay?"

"Well…yeah."

As much as I wanted to, I didn't look at him. I sliced through the box neatly. "Well, I like guys. Breasts don't do it for me. Soft bodies don't do it for me. I mean,

Peyton smells nice…but nothing that gets me going. Now, guys?" This time I did cast him a glance.

He watched me intently.

"I like how guys smell. I like their lower voices. Their angles." Their asses. Best not give away too much. "I can't explain it. I just…I'm attracted to guys. Not to girls."

"Right."

Very unhelpful. "But then you can look at someone like Peyton."

"Right."

"She doesn't care about a partner's gender. Some people say that true bisexuality doesn't exist, but Peyton's proof it does. She gets to know the person and decides if she's attracted to them based on their personality—not what's between their legs."

"Oh." He frowned. "Gets to know them first…"

"Well, she's not exactly demi. Just…if she's going to make out with someone, she needs to be attracted to them in more ways than just physical."

"Whereas you'll make out with any guy?"

I burst out laughing. "Uh, well. I'd say the guy needs to be gay. And have decent hygiene. Some of the most attractive guys in school…well, I want to suggest they take a shower."

Oliver snickered, then nabbed a handful of pasta boxes.

One more than I could hold at a time.

Bastard. Just has to be better at everything.

"You know who I'm talking about, right?"

"Yeah." He scrunched his nose. "Funky. Do you think it's a medical condition?"

I shook my head. "He's anti-shower. I don't know

how he gets away with it. And with that gorgeous hair? How it doesn't get greasy, I'll never understand."

"It kind of blows in the breeze."

"Right. He'd be so much more attractive if he just…I don't know…used deodorant?"

"Real." He put the older pasta on the shelf. "That it?"

"Yeah."

"Great."

Only as I walked home did I wonder about Oliver's *hair blowing in the breeze* comment.

Chapter Ten

Oliver

I might've been exhausted when I got home, but when I saw Aunt Leslie and Uncle Jeremiah sitting at the kitchen table, I felt guilty.

Still, Aunt Leslie rose to give me a hug. "I'm glad you're home safe. We could've come to get you."

"I had my bike, and it wasn't that far. Now…dead of winter and I might take you up on that offer."

Aunt Leslie laughed. "Raleigh might get more snow than Portland but way less than DC. Be glad we're not there." She appeared to think about it. "But we'll get more since we're in the mountains. It'll be interesting to see how much snow we get. Like I said, better than DC."

Flashing to Juliette, Peyton, and Holden, I realized I was super glad I wasn't there. "Uh, yeah, that's great."

"I'm boiling some water for chamomile tea." Uncle Jeremiah hovered his hands over two mugs.

"Sure, I'll take one." This had become our ritual on Monday nights. He didn't go into the office in Raleigh on Mondays, Tuesdays, and Thursdays—instead he was out visiting clients. That way, he didn't have to deal with the early morning rush hour. Generally, he spent Wednesdays and Fridays in the office. "No early morning?" I waved as my aunt turned toward the doorway. "Good night, Aunt Leslie."

She hesitated. "You know just Leslie is fine, right? I'm not that much older than you." Her smile was soft and didn't light her eyes. Likely, she was thinking about Mom.

"Aren't full titles the *southern way*?"

"But I'm not southern." She pointed to Uncle Jeremiah. "He is. Night." She headed out of the kitchen. Her light footfalls on the hardwood stairs carried through to me.

When she was truly gone, Uncle Jeremiah let out a breath. Sometimes, I could think of him as just Jeremiah. Like when he treated me like one of the guys instead of a nephew needing coddling.

He grinned. "I'd offer you something to make the tea go down smoother…"

"But Aunt Leslie will figure it out." I held my breath, just in case she was listening at the top of the stairs. When no response came, I let it out.

"Yeah." That grin turned gentler. "She's a good woman."

"That she is." I grabbed a couple of slices of processed cheese out of the fridge and sat at the kitchen table.

"She only buys that processed stuff for you. You know that right?" He winced. "Just…blech."

I laughed. He and Aunt Leslie were total health-food people. Still, I sought the right words. "Mom was always so busy that she used to toss a couple of slices my way while she prepared dinner." I blinked. "I think of her when I eat these."

"Which is why Leslie buys them and doesn't razz you about eating them. I think your grandmother told her a while back?" He frowned. "They had a long conversation about you a few years ago. Leslie took copious notes. Pulled out that notebook when we discovered you were coming to live with us. Overjoyed," he added.

I liked how he said *live with us* instead of just *stay with us*. He made it sound like a forever thing. Which it was. At least until I went to college. And *overjoyed*? Was there anything better to hear for a kid who'd lost everything?

He placed a mug of steaming tea before me but didn't warn me the mug was hot. The dirty look I'd given him the first two times had likely assured him I could tell the difference between a hot drink and a cold one.

I dunked the tea bag over and over, watching the light color slowly seep into the plain water.

Jeremiah nudged me. "Why are you so sad, dude? What can I do to help?"

Him calling me *dude* brought a smile to my face because my uncle was the least *dudebro* guy I knew. Finally, after a long pause, I met his gaze. "You work for the IRS, right?"

He slowly nodded. "I do. I don't tell people that I do, though. Some folks don't take kindly to me being an agent. People treat me differently. They think I can get them in trouble, even though I really can't. Unless I *know* they're doing something illegal."

I laughed. "Okay, I promise not to tell anyone."

"That's good." He pulled his tea bag out and dropped it onto a little saucer. "So what's this about? You thinking of becoming an agent? As I move up the ladder, I'm making better money. Government jobs come with good benefits and decent retirement packages. Just…you can be laid off and hired back depending on the whim of whoever's in the White House and whoever's running Congress."

Honestly, I hadn't thought about that. "Is there any job you can't be fired from?"

He squinted, as if in deep thought. "There must be. Like, maybe Pope? Just about everyone can be brought down." He snapped his fingers. "Queen of England. Well, King now. You can't depose a monarch." He cocked his head. "Well, I suppose you could mount a coup. Although there's already representative government…" He waved his hand. "I think you get the idea. You can be indispensable but rarely invincible." He sipped his tea. "Why are you asking about my job? Seriously, if you're interested in auditing, we can figure out a good career path. There are some great business schools—"

Me raising my hand stopped him. Abruptly. I winced inwardly, worrying I'd been too rude.

He grinned. "Okay, so no business school?"

I'd always planned to study architecture at the College of Design. The University of Oregon, of course. I had already sent my application package. Way earlier than necessary, but I didn't figure I'd be docked marks for enthusiasm. I supposed I should be looking at schools out here since I was no longer a resident of Oregon. Out-of-state tuition was beyond anything I could ask Aunt Leslie and Uncle Jeremiah to pay—even if they could afford it. "Keeping my options open…"

"Sounds good." He pointed to my mug, indicating I might want to drink it before it cooled.

Obediently, I took a sip. The soothing liquid slid down easily. I'd get drowsy soon, which helped me sleep. I didn't have the nightmares from after my parents first died, but I didn't love going to sleep either. These days, I worried my grandmother might pass. During the day, I could accept death was an inevitability, but at night, I couldn't keep the bad dreams at bay.

"Now, why the questions about my job if you're not interested? Is there a *bring your parent to school* day I didn't hear about?" He laughed.

"In high school? No, we don't do that anymore. And anyway, Mom was way cooler." I blinked.

"Yeah, she was." He reached for my hand. "Whatever you need, okay?"

"Okay." I cleared my throat. "Uh, do you know how to make fake IDs?"

He tilted his head but didn't release my hand. "What?"

"Could you make me a fake identity if you had to? I mean you know how to find them—to spot them—so it must mean you know how to make them. Right?"

"Yeah, I could. But why? You in trouble?" His grip on my hand tightened, and his expression turned serious with a little furrow in his brow. "What's wrong?"

"Nothing."

He continued to hold my gaze.

No fooling him. "Really. It's just that…I don't know…maybe I want to disappear?"

"Why?"

"You see…" *How am I supposed to tell him this? He's family, but in other ways, I barely know him.* I drew in a deep breath. "I like this person, but what if I tell them and they laugh at me? And what if they tell everyone and the entire school laughs at me?"

"Oh." Jeremiah squeezed my hand. "Okay, let's unpack this slowly. First, do you really care what other people think? If kids laugh at you—which would be horrible—would that be the end of the world?"

He knew me. I didn't want to give a shit what other people thought. I only wanted to care about how it might reflect on him and Aunt Leslie. The kids at school, though? "Uh, not really…"

"And so, what if this person laughs at you?"

"It…" Another deep breath. "I think it would hurt my feelings."

"Yeah. But you know your aunt and I will be here for you? That we'll support you. No matter what." He sipped his tea. "It's getting cold."

"I know you'll support me." I managed a smile. I *did* know.

"Okay." After one last squeeze, he released my hand. "So why don't you tell me about this girl?"

"Uh…"

Uncle Jeremiah arched an eyebrow. "Oh." He cleared his throat. "Oh…well…that's cool. Why don't you tell me about…whomever. I won't judge, Oliver. I promise. Your aunt and I are…accepting. Okay? No matter what."

I wanted to make some kind of stupid joke, but his earnestness spoke to me. Still, having his understanding meant everything. "He's…" I hesitated. "Funny? Sarcastic? Brave…"

"He sounds like a great guy. I'm listening, and I want to hear all about him."

"Uh…he's great. I mean, super cute and funny." I suppressed a yawn. "He takes care of his younger sister and watches out for his mom." I thought some more. "He defends kids who aren't as strong as him. And I don't mean physically. He just…he's out and so gutsy."

"He sounds like a very special young man."

I blinked. "He kind of is. And I don't think he looks at me in *that* way, you know?"

"But you wish he would."

"Maybe? I mean, I know how tough it is for gay kids."

Jeremiah offered a sympathetic smile. "Yes, for sure. You have my support. Our support. If you want to say something to other people, that's fine. If you want to keep it just between us for now, that's okay too. You need to be true to what feels right. Are you worried this boy might reject you?"

I spun my mug ninety degrees. "Yeah."

He cleared his throat. "That's something we all go through, I think. Both worrying about rejection and, I fear, being rejected. Don't think that just because I'm happy now that I didn't go through a few bumpy patches."

"You and Aunt Leslie?" Maybe I should've been able to, but I honestly couldn't fathom it. They were just so happy together. So damn in love with each other. I wanted that. Perhaps sooner rather than later.

He held my gaze. "Is it okay if I tell your aunt, or do you want me to wait for you to tell her?"

"No. I mean, it's fine. I'll talk to both of you. I would never ask you to keep a secret from her."

Jeremiah yawned.

As an empathetic yawner, I did as well. "I think we need to go to bed."

He grinned, then downed the rest of his tea.

Mine remained virtually untouched. But after a long evening stocking shelves, I was exhausted.

We rose at the same time.

He held my gaze. "Are we good?"

"Yeah."

He smiled at my using his favorite word. "Hug it out? Or is that too weird?"

I stepped into his embrace—feeling safe for the first time since my grandma started to lose her memory. "I love you."

"We love you too."

Chapter Eleven

Juliette

I eyed Duncan even as my calculus text sat before me, commanding me to pay attention. "So you died fighting in the Civil War?"

He gave me the nineteenth-century version of *duh* with his expression. Sarcastically raised eyebrow and all.

"Well, you might've died after the war." I floundered. "Although, admittedly, with your uniform, that feels less likely. Although they could've buried you in it."

"As the kids these days say…what is it again? Oh. *Keep digging.*"

I giggled. "You must know so many expressions."

He sighed. "You have no idea. It's been a long…journey."

"Okay, but, like, can you move on?"

"Move on?" Now his expression turned into a frown. "There is no *moving on.* I am to walk the Earth until it ends."

"Like life on the planet? Because if we keep pumping carbon dioxide and other pollutants that cause climate change, we're going to make the planet uninhabitable—"

He held up his hand. "Do you not believe civilization will remedy that before it happens?"

"Have you met our politicians?" This time, I frowned. "They don't listen to us—even though we're the ones who have to live here. Climate disasters all over the world don't change their attitudes."

"Can't you…" He tapped his chin. "Lobby the politicians?"

I snorted. "I promise you, big industry, big corporations, and big oil all got there first. I can join the environmental club and clean up the banks for the river, but that's only a drop in the bucket."

"Yes, but many drops fill that bucket."

I opened my mouth to argue…then shut it. "That's, like, profound."

He snickered—possibly a response to my very unladylike snort or possibly because he'd clearly brought me up short. "I've had over one hundred years to perfect my profundity."

"Is that even a word?" I'd never heard it although my parents insisted I read widely during every school vacation to increase my linguistic prowess. Ha! I wanted to go to summer camp and, when I was older, be a counselor. But nope, reading books all during the vacations for me. A couple of trips to Europe thrown in. To increase my *worldliness.*

"If it isn't a word, it should be. Now…calculus…"

"You can't help me, can you?"

He hesitated. "I sit in on literature, history, and geography classes. Dissecting frogs, determining the speed of light, and difficult mathematical calculations are of no interest to me."

"What would you have liked to be? If not a soldier." I twirled my pencil.

After a long moment, he sighed. "At the time of my

death, my ambition was to free other slaves. I don't know how I could have done that—I didn't have the education for politics, or the skin color, and I wasn't the bold sort to steal them from their owners. But that desire burned inside me. Now? I'd like to be a teacher. English, I think. And, perhaps, even a scholar. A teacher who teaches teachers." He chuckled. "An ambition far beyond my reach."

"Only because you died." I eyed him. "I think you could've achieved greatness—if not for the dying thing."

"Ah, yes, the *dying thing*." He pursed his lips. "Puts a crimp in one's style."

I burst out laughing. "You did *not* just say that."

"Oh, I most certainly did." He shrugged. "I didn't attend school in my lifetime. I've spent a century attempting to learn here. I want to be a learned man. But what would I do with this talent? Teach other ghosts? To what end? It's not like we're going somewhere."

"Okay, but that's my point."

He scowled.

I ignored him and continued. "What if, I don't know…you have some kind of task you need to complete on Earth before you move on? I mean…are you in purgatory? Somewhere between Heaven and Hell?"

"I…" He cleared his throat.

Which always struck me as funny.

"I used to believe in Heaven and Hell. Sinners and saints. My existence beyond death has taught me that, if such places exist, I am not destined to be there."

"Okay, but have any other ghosts left and not come back? Or are you all condemned to wander the halls and never leave? Because, frankly, that would suck. Slightly better than being stuck in the factory, I suppose. There, all you'd hear is gossip. Here, there are minds. Exchanges of idea."

He rolled his eyes.

"You know what I mean."

"I do." He stretched his fingers. "If I could've chosen anywhere, I would've selected a university library. Or, even better, an entire university. Although, as you say, there are worse places. I'd dread being in a first-grade classroom."

I burst out laughing. "Yeah, I can see you're not the nurturing type."

He put his hands on his hips. "I enjoy nurturing. I'm just better at doing it with adults."

"Right." I glanced at my phone. "We're getting off track. Tasks for ghosts?"

"I have no idea. We defeated the rebels—the Confederates. The Union was victorious. The Yankees won. What more would there be beyond that?"

I tapped my pencil on my long-forgotten calculus textbook.

"They also killed me, Juliette, so I really don't think I'm going to be able to come alive and kill them back. Just sayin'."

I snickered. "Oh, you do have fun."

"Groovy was a word I had a particular affinity for."

"See, you use big words. Maybe you *can* teach the other ghosts."

"To what end? So we can have erudite discussions about history, world politics, and…literature?" He shrugged. "I've tried to talk to Willie…but he always runs away."

"Who's Willie?"

"Another ghost. I should've befriended him sooner.

I think he might be lonely. Although, he appears to have made a friend who visits the library daily to spend time with him. I'm tempted to listen in—"

"But you won't because you're respectful of other people's privacy."

He huffed.

I laughed. Then sobered. "But there must be *something* you can do to change your fate."

"No, I do not believe so. This is my eternal state."

"Uh, do all people become ghosts? Because it seems to me the world would be awfully crowded."

He appeared to contemplate his answer. "I don't know. Many who have died on school grounds appear to have remained as ghosts. Why me and not my companions, I am uncertain."

"Right…but are there ghosts who died before the school was established?"

"Well…"

I rolled my hand, hoping he'd take the hint and hurry up.

"The Indigenous people of this area had a burial site. That's being excavated. Which you know. And undoubtedly you heard about the imported castle remains. Fiona belongs to that part of history. She's been here for centuries. Although Mary has been here longer. She was escaping the Salem Witch trials when she came south. She died and was buried by her friends near the native burial ground, which was, of course, here long before the first settlers."

"Oh, I hadn't thought of that. They wouldn't have found the ruins if they hadn't been expanding the football field and the bleachers." I tapped my pencil. "So if everyone stays, you should see Native ghosts and maybe more castle ghosts?"

"Well, very few people die on burial sites. They die elsewhere and are brought there."

"Huh…never thought of it like that. Just like you don't usually die *in* a cemetery. They bring you to one after."

"There are Indigenous spirits." He gazed outside.

Is he seeing one now? Wouldn't that be so cool? Still, I was lucky to be in the presence of one ghost. How would I cope with a whole pile of them? I scribbled Duncan's name in the margin of my notebook. "What's your last name?"

"I'm not certain that's relevant."

"Humor me." I met his gaze head-on.

"Galloway."

"Okay."

"What do you intend to do with that information?"

"Oh, you know, this and that…"

He scowled. "I do not know what *this and that* is."

"I have access to a bunch of websites. Like for ancestors. People build family trees and stuff. You might be on one of them. Did you ever have children?"

Something flashed in his eyes. There one minute— gone the next. Nothing I could identify in words.

"I do not believe so, no."

"Was there a woman—"

The classroom door swung open.

Peyton strolled in. "Hey, there you are." She craned her neck to see my book. "You need help?"

"From you? Always."

At the whistling sound, I turned back to where Duncan had been.

Gone.

I spun back to Peyton. "Did you see him?"

She blinked. "When I came in here, you were alone. Did you…did you think there was someone in here with you?"

"Of course not." But he would've still been here when she walked in, so either she hadn't noticed him or, much more likely, she hadn't seen him. I scribbled *Galloway* next to *Duncan* and closed my notebook. "I'm out of time for calculus, though. Can I walk you to biology?" Her class was down the hall from the physics classroom.

"Sure." She grinned that goofy grin that I loved— *liked* so much. "Oliver's in your class, right?"

I nodded as I scooped up my books and rose. *So much for getting studying done.* I probably should've chosen another spot, but I enjoyed my conversations with Duncan. And by his own admission, he could go anywhere in the school. I glanced at Peyton…which involved looking down a bit. I loved her short stature— just made the fact she was willing to stand up to the bullies all the more incredible. "Are you ready for tonight's game?"

She grinned and indicated I should exit the door before her.

So polite. And kickass. Nice combination.

"You bet. I swapped out my reed—which you did not need to know. I'm all practiced up and ready."

We strolled leisurely, letting the other students weave around us.

"You really love music."

She grinned. "I do. I volunteer in an after-school program to teach basic music skills to little kids when the band's not in full swing. Which excludes football season,

112

basketball season, volleyball season…plus graduations, parades, and other events. We stay busy for a good chunk of the year." She offered me a cheeky smile. "Most of which you know because of cheer squad."

"It's weird we haven't—"

"Can we study—"

I indicated she should go first.

"Can we study again this weekend? I mean, I'm sure you've got better—"

"Nope."

She faltered.

"Oh. No, I don't have anything better to do. Yes, we can study. My house or yours?" *Okay, maybe try to play it cool?*

"Your house doesn't have weird mom vibes."

I laughed. "Your mom's okay."

"She can be…a little much." She scrunched her face in a super-cute way. "What were you going to say earlier?"

"Just that it's weird we've never had classes together."

"We did." She stared up at me. "Several over the past three years."

Heat flooded my cheeks, and I fervently prayed she couldn't see my embarrassment. "Oh."

"It's okay." She reached out as if to touch me, then pulled back at the last moment. "You're a cheerleader. I'm a band player. Those two sets of people aren't exactly known for mixing."

"But you and Holden are so great."

Her eyes widened.

Crap. Too enthusiastic? "I'm just saying I wish I'd gotten to know you sooner. Because, I mean, school is

113

almost over."

She snickered. "Juliette? It's the beginning of October. Unless you're finished after fall semester, we have about nine months to go."

Duh. "Right…I just meant…you know, college and stuff." *Like I'll probably never see you again.*

"You okay?"

"Of course. Just…you know…"

"You keep saying that. Which is very unlike you."

"Oh, look, this is my classroom. I know I said I'd walk you to yours, but it's just down the hall, and I wouldn't want to be late." *Even though we have nine minutes.* I slowly backed away. "Bye."

Then I turned and practically ran into the room.

Chapter Twelve

Willie

"Hey." I wanted to nudge Duncan's shoulder as I sat next to him on the bleacher, but as a ghost, I couldn't touch him. October was unseasonably warm this year, and I desperately wished I could feel the sun beating down on my face. I missed warmth even more than I missed cold.

"Hello." He cocked his head. "You don't usually come out here when no one is around."

"You noticed that, eh? I prefer watching the games, of course. I mean I can't sit in the bleachers, but there's a quiet spot off on that hill." I pointed. "Today, though...nostalgic. Is that the right word? Thinking about all the games I watched here."

"I've watched a few over the years. Of course, we didn't have football in my day. Very violent sport."

I rolled my eyes. "Duncan, you fought in a literal war. Football is nothing compared to that." *Was that too forward? Will he take offense?*

"William."

My gut clenched. Ever since he'd wheedled out of me that my name was officially William and not Willie, he insisted on calling me it. Funny how I'd never told anyone and then in the space of just a couple of weeks had told both Holden and Duncan. "What?"

He cleared his throat.

Whenever he did that, I wondered if his throat had been slit as a way to kill him. Or had he been bayonetted in the windpipe? I didn't want to imagine how he died…but I was intensely curious. "Yes…"

"I was speaking to Juliette."

"Oh, the cheer captain? She's a lovely woman. Attractive. Sweet. Doesn't swear." *Like me*. Sometimes I purposefully observed students who didn't curse to learn new creative ways to swear without using foul language. She was a fun one to follow around.

"As you say." Duncan cleared his throat again.

Does he think she's attractive? They'd make a handsome couple. Him all tall and proud in his uniform. Her in that silver dress she wore to the formal last year… Yeah, I could totally see them together. Except for the corporeal-noncorporeal thing. That made life challenging. "What's up, D?"

"D?" He frowned. "My name is Duncan. Corporal Duncan Jeremiah Galloway of the Massachusetts 54th. I am not, nor have I ever been, nor will I ever be, D."

Sheesh. "Okay."

"And I believe you should be William. Not Willie. Not Billy. Not even Liam…although that is an acceptable name. William."

Lord save me from this guy.

Yet still, I didn't leave. "I'm William and you're Duncan. Got it. Now can we finally discuss whatever is on your mind?"

He frowned, almost as if he'd lost the thread of the conversation.

"Juliette," I prompted.

"Oh, right." He offered me a small smile.

Ha! He does like her. That made me a little sad, but I'd get over it. God knew I had nothing else to do with my time.

"She has a theory."

"Juliette?"

"Yes. I just said that. Pay attention, William. Get with the program."

I resisted the urge to stick my tongue out at him. Barely. "Right…theory…"

"Yes, she believes we are here for a reason. That we have some kind of mission. And that once we complete that task, we can move on to…wherever we're meant to move on to."

"Like Heaven or Hell."

He winced. "I'm not certain I would put it so crassly."

"Too blunt for you?"

"Well, yes, possibly." He shifted. "What do you think of her theory?"

I glanced down at myself, completely naked. Even if I couldn't feel the wind in my hair and the sun on my skin, I wanted to believe I might tan. Pasty white—even while alive—hadn't been a good look. "I have no idea. You, I could perhaps understand. You might have some greater purpose. Some higher calling. Something that they—whoever *they* are—need you to do. But then why the hell am I stuck here? There's nothing that I left uncompleted on Earth. I was only seventeen. I mean, I should've come out of the closet, of course. Being a coward in my life really gets to me. But what is the good of coming out now?"

Duncan looked toward the field for a long time before focusing his gaze on me. "How did you die?"

"Slipping in the shower. I told you."

"Slipped." His eyes narrowed.

"Someone walked in, and I had to turn, you know, suddenly."

"Why? Were they going to perv on you? Interestingly, although that word has been around for over six hundred years, I only recently learned it." He frowned. "Well *to pervert* has been around for six hundred years. *Pervert* in the sexual sense is slightly younger."

"How much is *slightly*?"

"Sixteen sixty or so."

"Older than Mary."

"Older than Mary."

"Wow." I waved my hand. "And now you've gotten me off track. No one was going to perv on me." *I only wish they were—*

"What?"

I squinted. "What, what? I said no one was going to perv on me."

"But you said something after that."

"No, I didn't." *I didn't say that out loud…did I? Oh, can he hear my thoughts?* "Uh, what was I just thinking?"

His eyes widened. "Thinking? Unless you speak your thoughts aloud, how could I possibly know what you are thinking? Are you mad?"

"Uh…drat. You weren't meant to hear that."

"Hear what?"

Go for broke. "That I wished the guy would've perved on me."

Duncan closed his eyes for a moment, as if in thought. "You're still hung up on this guy, aren't you?

This kid from over thirty years ago?"

Thirty-five…but who's counting? "Hung up? Well…" I took a deep breath. "I'm surprised you didn't notice him, D. Sorry, Duncan." I winced inwardly but kept going. "He was so gorgeous. Fit and handsome and everything I ever wanted. He was…perfect."

Duncan snickered. "No one is perfect. You were in love with the ideal. Not the real. You were young and idealistic—"

"I was seventeen!"

"Exactly my point."

"What, and at twenty you knew everything about the world?" I waved him off before he could get started. I had a good head of steam going, and I was going to continue. "I loved him, okay? And I know guys didn't exactly get together back then…or at least I didn't know any who did. But I'd heard of the AIDS crisis. So I knew guys had…" I gulped and spun my hand.

"Had sex with other guys?" Duncan offered an amused look.

Which should've offended me, but I couldn't use the *actual words* to describe what I wanted to describe. So he was, in fact, helping me. "Right. But, I don't know, maybe in college we could've gotten together. Or, like, after college. He was a big guy on the football field. Captain of the team. Quarterback, of course. He had the sexiest body, and I might have been thinking about him—" *Stop talking. Stop talking. Stop talking.*

"When he walked in on you in the shower?" More amusement.

Ghosts didn't blush. That much I'd learned. In real life, though, I would've been fire-engine red. "Maybe…"

Duncan sighed. "When you've been through thick

119

and thin with a man and still love him, even after you've seen the depths of his soul, then you get to say he was ideal. All you say about this football guy is that he was nice-looking."

"Well, he was."

My unearthly companion scratched his chin.

Does his skin itch? Mine never does. "What are you thinking?"

He shrugged. "Just that, after all this time, perhaps you might consider letting him go."

"Did you ever *love* someone? See into the *depths of their soul*?"

"In fact, I had two great loves."

I goggled. "You were twenty, and you loved two people? Did they know about each other?"

He smiled. "We were living in a time of war. Things were different back then." His expression turned wistful, his eyes a little unfocused. "I loved a woman deeply. We married a week before I was sent south with my regiment. We wrote, but…" He hesitated. "I believe she met someone else. She spoke of there being another *man* in her life. In the end, I died. So it didn't matter."

"Okay. That's one person. Super sad, but one person."

The smile he offered me was now rueful. "I fell in love with someone else I became close with. Not in the same way I loved my wife, but close nonetheless."

I wagged my finger at him. "So you cheated on her."

He pressed a hand to his chest. "I would never."

"What was her name?"

"My wife? Esmeralda."

"And the name of the woman you loved after leaving your wife at home?"

He smiled that enigmatic smile I was becoming so familiar with. "Elijah."

My jaw dropped. "Care to repeat that?"

"Certainly. I…what's the word the kids use? Had a crush on Elijah. Who was in love and had a relationship—albeit a secret one—with Cornelius."

"Three gay men in the regiment?" I pondered that.

"Perhaps more. But I didn't tell him. Didn't act on my attraction. As well, if we're insisting on labels, I am bisexual. I had powerful attractions to both men and women. I would've been happy living with my wife for the rest of my life, and if something happened to her and I found myself alone, I would've been just as happy with Elijah. Or satisfied, I would say."

"Had you been with other men before?"

He nodded. "Several. It might've been against the law, but so was being with a prostitute. Other *sins* as well. Adultery being a big one. I might've lain with men on occasion before my marriage, but I would never have cheated on my wife."

"Well, that's something." I tried to puff out my chest. A weak attempt at best since I didn't have breath to expand my lungs. *I really wish I'd had a growth spurt* before *I died.* And then, *if wishes were pennies, I'd be rich.* Thirty-five years as a spirit had led to many, many, many wishes. Things left undone. Unsaid. Family I missed terribly. My parents would die in the next few decades. My little sister's seizures had kept her from coming here, and instead, she'd been homeschooled. I might've done better if I could've seen her every day.

Or not.

Time to stop looking back. "What are your plans for this evening?" In the time we'd been out here, the sun had dipped lower in the sky. The marshmallow-puffy clouds tinged pink in the waning light. A light breeze whipped the trees.

"Red at night, sailor's delight." He paused. "Red in the morning, sailor's warning."

I cocked my head. "I'm assuming that's a real saying."

"It is."

"And is it true?"

He shrugged. "I don't have empirical data either way. Maybe I could convince someone to search it on one of those fancy devices…"

"Computers?"

"Or phones. I've gone from watching the Teletype, to the telephone, to the internet, and now cell phones."

I squinted. "Yeah, only landlines before I died. I would love to try a cell phone out. Just to see all the things they can do these days."

Duncan rose. "I shall bid you good night. I am off to the history classroom for a while."

Which sounded incredibly boring to me. Nothing to do up there.

Except be alone. "Hey, I can leave—you were here first." Him wanting to be away from me hurt a little, but I could respect him.

He shrugged. "If you've seen one sunset…" He gestured toward the sky. "Nice to see you, William."

"Willie."

He gazed at me.

I didn't miss the wince. He really didn't like my shortened name. "Yeah, see you around."

With that, he descended the bleachers and headed back across the field and toward the school.

As night set in, I sat and watched the stars emerge. I'd been to Raleigh a bunch of times. Had even taken a trip to Washington DC once. I didn't like the bright lights or the big city. I was happy in my corner of the universe. If I could leave now, however, I certainly would.

That was a contradiction I never chose to examine closely, because leaving was impossible.

And so I stayed.

Chapter Thirteen

Holden

I sought Willie out on the Wednesday after Columbus Day. Or Indigenous People's Day, as some people called it. I was all for traditions, but not at the expense of celebrating someone who, in the passing of time, had become problematic. That being said, I was still proud to be an American. I'd done some research, and the Canadian Indigenous people called Canada *Turtle Island*. Which made me wonder how those inhabitants, before Europeans landed on the shores, viewed their home. Oh, and Vikings had landed in Newfoundland and created a settlement in 1021 CE. But that didn't fit with the narrative of Columbus being the first, so we often ignored the clear historical evidence.

Way too far down the rabbit hole.

I discovered my favorite naked ghost hanging out by the foreign-language books.

He grinned as I approached.

"Don't you ever wish you could open a book and read?" I hesitated. "Or can you open a book? Do you have, I don't know, levitation powers or something?"

"Those happen to be two different things. Every ghost is different. I am stuck walking everywhere I want to go. You'd think I could levitate—or wish myself somewhere and then find myself there. Alas, that's not me."

"Did you just say *alas*?" I chuckled.

He squinted. "I went through a Shakespeare phase a few years ago. Sat in all the English classes. I watched all the movies they showed, soaked up the lectures. Heck, the school even did a version of *Romeo and Juliet*."

I snapped my fingers. "I remember that. I was in eighth grade and was bundled off with my classmates to see the show. It felt very bloodthirsty."

"Right." He waved excitedly. "Although, really, Macbeth takes the award for most ghoulish."

"Yes. That washing-blood-off-hands thing was kind of gross."

"You know she didn't *actually* have blood on her hands."

I rolled my eyes. "No, she didn't. But just the idea that she'd committed murder freaked me out."

He waved me off. "You think women can't murder? Can't slaughter innocents? If I told you—" He winced. "Oh, shit—" Then he clapped his hand over his mouth. He uttered, "Drat," from behind his fingers.

"Did you just—" I gasped. "—swear?"

"No." A typical Willie squeak.

"Dude, that's awesome. I didn't think we'd ever get there."

He put his hands on his slender hips, emphasizing the fact he was naked.

I will not look down. I will not look down. I will… Yeah, wasn't going to comment on *that*. "Swearing is cool."

"You think you're grown up because you use expletives? Makes you look…uh…"

"I'm one of your few friends…careful how you insult me." Of course, I wasn't going anywhere. "Wait…am I your only friend?"

He pursed his lips. "You're the only living person who's ever seen me."

"And you don't consider that just a little bit weird?"

"I was just so grateful that I haven't questioned it."

I gave him my patented *are you shitting me* look.

"All right, I've spent lots of time thinking about it. But I worried if I overthought it, you might no longer be able to see me. That the…beings…who control all this might revoke my privileges."

I straightened. "I'm a privilege?" I kind of liked the sound of that.

He tilted his head from one side to the other. "Frankly, I'm not certain what you are."

"A friend."

"Yes. Just like Juliette is Duncan's friend."

"Duncan?"

"A Civil War soldier."

"A ghost?"

"Yeah."

My brain screeched to a halt—like a needle scratching on my friend's old record player. "You mean I'm not the only one who can see ghosts?"

"Well, you're the only one who can see me." He pursed his lips yet again.

I found the gesture endearing. Cute. Still not attracted to him, but he was growing on me.

"I don't know why she can see Duncan."

"I should talk—"

"No." He elongated the O. "Let's just leave things as they are. Status quo."

I wanted to protest—meeting a Civil War dude would be awesome, and I was super curious whether we could see each other's ghosts—but I had to respect Willie's obvious fear. "Okay. Now you made me forget why I came in here."

"That's okay." He appeared to think about it. "Well, I mean, not okay. I mean if it was important, then I hope you remember. Were you going to ask me something? Oh, were you going to ask me a favor? Because I'd love to do you a favor. Not that I can do much. But you know—"

Holding up my hand appeared to effectively end his monologue as he shut his mouth. "Whatever I thought I needed to talk about clearly wasn't that important. So…did you have something on your mind?" I had a sixth sense something was up with him today.

He pulled his lower lip through his teeth.

Does he feel that? Does he realize what he's doing? I wasn't going to ask in case I derailed him.

"I need you to do something for me." He appeared to be trying to put on a brave face.

I wouldn't laugh at his seriousness—much as I wanted to. "Sure, what?"

"Can you find out what happened to Frank Fletcher? He was captain of the football team here. In 1989."

"Uh, sure. That's it?" I eyed him. "Why am I doing this?"

"Can't you just—" He waved vaguely toward my back pocket. "—type his name into your phone, and it comes up?"

"Sure…" I held his gaze as I yanked out my phone. I typed in everything, and the search had results right away. I frowned. *Does he really want to know this? Well,*

127

he's a grown man. Sort of. He's... My mind stuttered. I loved math, but... "You're, what, fifty-two?"

He glared impatiently. "Yes. What's your point?"

"Just making certain it's the same Frank Fletcher." *And stalling for time because I think this is going to hurt you.* Finally, after drawing a deep breath, I held out the phone. "You sure this is him? I mean, ew. He can't be the guy you loved, can it?" Yet even as I asked the question, I knew the answer. "This is his mug shot. He beat up his wife."

Willie held still for a long moment.

I had to tap the screen again so it wouldn't go dark.

"I have to go." He spun and walked out of the library. That weird whistling sound followed him.

Well, okay then. I let out a long breath, hefted my backpack, put my phone back into my pocket, and headed to English class.

I nearly told Peyton about Willie. Partly because I needed reassurances and partly because I wanted to know if she saw ghosts as well. But she'd tell me, right?

Except you haven't told her.

I scowled at my inner voice.

English class flew by in a blur of Hamlet, soliloquies, and deaths. My only question was, why didn't Horatio—the only one left standing—get to be king? Why did some dude from a far-off land get the privilege? Something about only kings being able to rule, Ms. Cracken explained.

Calling bullshit wouldn't earn me any favors. Several times, I glanced around the room. Willie had once said he could travel anywhere on school grounds. That he preferred the library. That's why I always found him there. Really, though, I'd never looked for him elsewhere. Today I did. As well as wondering if I might spot other ghosts.

I didn't. And wound up back in the library for my spare period.

Said period was nearly half over when Willie approached me.

Being prudent, I'd headed to foreign languages again. Never had company there.

Willie sat on the floor, much as he had that first day. I joined him.

"I was…" He wiped at his cheeks even though I didn't see tears.

Because ghosts don't cry…right?

Yeah, that's what you're focusing on?

"How are you doing?"

"I went to the locker room."

One of my least favorite places. Funky smell and bullies liked to hang out there. So one of the places in school I avoided at all costs now that I was a senior and didn't have compulsory PE. Still, I had to try. "Yeah?"

"And I was thinking. Remembering all the horrible things he used to say to the younger kids—including myself. He was…a bully. And then I thought, *what a fucker.*"

I held in the laughter at his finally swearing, but didn't speak because he needed to work this out for himself.

"Duncan was right." He sighed.

"How so?"

"He said I was in love with the ideal. That the real Frank wasn't the person I loved. I thought he was just blowing smoke up my—" He squinted. "Nope, not going to say it."

"You thought Duncan was blowing smoke up your ass? That he was just saying something made up?"

"Yes." He laced his arms around his bent knees, encircling his legs. "How did this happen?"

"Well, you had no way of knowing Frank turned out to be a first-class asshole. I read that he lives in Palm Beach. So word clearly didn't filter back up here." I longed to reach out and feather his blond hair. So fine and a light color.

Willie blinked up at me. "How are things going with your crush?"

This time, I took my turn to sigh. "Well, every day I want him more and more. I think I'm falling in love with him."

"Are you worried you might be in love with an ideal?"

I scowled. "Well, I wasn't before." I blew out a breath. "Oliver will *never* wind up like your Frank."

"He's not *my* Frank. But…" He squinted. "I can, now, see the signs. Does your Oliver bully weaker kids?"

"Oh God, no. He stands up for weaker kids who get bullied. He's just…a really good guy. So, of course, that makes me love him more." The bell rang. "Okay, I need to run. You going to be okay?"

"Sure. Nothing's changed."

I gave him the side-eye.

"Well, okay. Like, everything's changed. Maybe…I should find Duncan, right? He's got to be around here somewhere." He waved me off. "Go love your guy. I hope it doesn't wind up being unrequited."

In the process of standing, I hesitated.

He offered a winsome smile. "Shakespeare."

"Right. Check out Ms. Cracken's classes this week."

"Thanks, I will."

He didn't appear as sad as when I'd first told him, but clearly the news had devastated him.

How would I feel if Oliver turned out to be an abuser?

My heart would break. Of that, I was certain.

Chapter Fourteen

Duncan

Something was wrong. I felt it in my bones. *Don't panic*. Even if a crisis was going on, nothing existed that I could do. Students milled around after school, but something compelled me to make my way to the locker room. The football team was already on the field, so the room was empty.

Except for Willie.

Who was holding his nose while blood spurted.

Ghosts don't bleed, do they? Admittedly, I'd never done anything that might make me bleed.

He hadn't spotted me as he grabbed a washcloth and held it against his nose. He sat on the bench.

"Are you all right? Is there something I can do?"

"My nose." He wailed the words in a way that almost made me laugh.

Almost.

"Really, William, what have you done?"

"It's Willie, and I think my nose is broken." He nearly choked as he breathed. "And I'm naked." Another wail.

"You've been naked for thirty-five…" Startled, I held off judgment until I could determine a full set of facts. "You breathed. Holy Christ, you're real."

"Yes." He clearly attempted to shoot daggers at me.

His beautiful blue eyes merely enchanted me. Another thought I'd unpack later. "Ghosts can't breathe."

"Duh." He continued to wheeze. "They can't break their noses either."

"Are you saying—" My mind reeled with the improbability of what I was witnessing. "—you're alive?"

"Again, duh. Duncan, you *really* need to help me. I might've been naked for thirty-five years, but I wasn't alive. I'm freezing cold and really don't want anyone to see me this way."

"Oh dear. I should—" I was cut off by the locker room door opening.

Hank, the janitor, pushed his way in with a rag and a bottle of cleaning fluid. "Well…" He cleared his throat. "This is awkward." His gaze moved between the two of us.

"I didn't do it." I held up my hands.

Hank chuckled. "Didn't think you did. Well, Willie, this is a predicament. How did you come back to life?" He put his cleaning supplies on the top of a locker. Then he advanced toward Willie. "Not really the time." He kneeled down before my friend.

And yes, I considered him a friend.

"I don't know," Willie wailed.

"You've obviously rematerialized."

I blinked. "That's not a thing."

"It's rare." Hank made the correction even as he continued to examine Willie. "We need to get you clothes and then off to see the athletic trainer. A nurse or doctor would be better, but we'll start with someone who can quickly tape up your nose."

"Won't the trainer realize he doesn't know William?"

To which I got another glare from my friend.

"Willie?" I frowned. "Sorry, I always revert back to formality in a time of crisis."

Hank glanced up and down my body. "Yeah, I'd say so."

I stood a little straighter. "Well, you don't have to get snippy."

He grinned. "You've always been a challenge." He pivoted back to Willie. "I know where I can get you some clothes." He hustled out of the room with due haste.

Willie removed the washcloth. "Seems a bit better."

"That's a relief." I pointed to the door. "The janitor—"

"So not the time, Duncan." He snagged a towel and laid it over his lap.

And for the first time, I understood his embarrassment. As a ghost, his nudity annoyed him. Now, though, he was clearly mortified.

Hank arrived back in short order, relieving me from having to say anything.

Because, really, what was there to say? I couldn't offer words of comfort. I couldn't even explain to him what had happened—because I didn't understand it myself.

"Let's take a look at that nose." Hank examined William's—Willie's—nose, probing gently. "I'm no expert, but I don't believe it's broken. You wash up, get dressed, and we'll reassess."

Willie held his clothes to his chest as he scurried away.

I eyed Hank. "You've had a lot of experience with

broken noses?" I wasn't trying to be snarky, and I winced as it came out that way. "Sorry."

"That's all right." He examined the blood-soaked washcloth, then tossed it into the trash. "I suppose I could try to save it, but it's pretty old anyway."

"Why were you commenting about me earlier? Have I done something to offend you?"

He snickered. "Duncan, I've been working here for years."

"Yes, but—"

He cleared his throat. "Now's not the time."

Of course, he was right. Willie reentered the room. He wore a sweatshirt that was a bit big and jeans that were a little small—which really didn't bother me—and shoes that fit just right.

I gave him a smile, pushing aside the puzzle of our janitor to focus on the man before me. "Are you okay?"

He drew in another breath, gently poking his nose. "Yeah, I think so. I thought I'd broken my nose…" He gave me a sheepish look. "I might wind up with a black eye, but I agree with Hank that it's not broken."

"Well, that's great." Hank started to leave.

"Wait," Willie cried out.

Hank stilled.

"I still need help."

"I don't think I can offer you the kind of help you're looking for." Hank grabbed his bottle of cleaning fluid and a rag. "I'm just going to—"

"Do you…" Willie gesticulated wildly.

Hank blinked.

As did I.

"I need…" Willie swallowed. "I can't exactly show up on my mother's doorstep."

"That's true." Hank gazed at me. "You should help him." With that, he stepped out of the room.

Willie dropped, clearly dejected, onto the bench. "How am I supposed to know what to do? And you? You're…ancient…"

Despite everything, I laughed. "I'm going to take that as a compliment."

"Oh, I didn't mean—"

"You have a breathing friend, right?"

"Uh…Holden? Yeah."

"Might you track him down and ask him for assistance?"

"Uh…I guess." He gazed upward to the ceiling, as if he were able to divine something from the fake tiles. "Today's Wednesday, right?"

"Well, the day before yesterday we didn't have students for company—and it was Columbus Day— that's a safe bet."

"Marching band practice."

"I suppose."

"You have to come with me."

"I suppose." I was trying to play it cool, even as I felt excitement grow within me. If Willie could rematerialize, might I also?

And what precisely did Hank know? Had he seen me all these years? I knew about his history, of course, but we'd never conversed. Today was proving to be fascinating.

I followed Willie out of the locker room, down the hall, and toward the band room. Every other Wednesday, a group of eighth grade students came to the school and practiced their instruments. Either Holden or Peyton—or sometimes both—stuck around to help the kids. I hadn't observed this pattern until Willie told me Holden could see him. I'd tried, on several occasions, to approach the young man. If Juliette could see me and Holden could see Willie, why not the inverse? Alas, he'd walked right past me.

Well, he'd hesitated for a moment, looked my way, then kept going.

Damn my life.

So to speak.

When we entered the band room, Holden was speaking to two young women in tight T-shirts, short skirts, and high heels.

Eighth grade?

Then I noted how they batted their eyelashes at Holden. Gave him starry-eyed glances. No one had ever looked at me like that—not even my eminently practical wife who had, I believed, adored me. I'd certainly loved her. Just as I'd cared for Elijah even as he'd had his Cornelius. I could understand coveting without acting on that attraction.

Clearly, these young women fancied Holden. Were they not aware he was too old for them? That he was out and gay? Or did that not matter?

Willie stood in the doorway, transfixed.

"Go." I whispered the word. "You need to talk to him." Why he didn't see the urgency of this situation, I was unclear.

"I know that, doofus." He hissed that back.

Doofus? Really? We certainly could have a conversation later. About time and place. He truly was a child of the eighties. The nineteen eighties, of course.

He cleared his throat.

Holden glanced up, held up a finger as if to indicate

for Willie to wait a moment, then he returned his attention to the young women. "You really need to practice to improve."

One twirled a lock of hair between her fingers. "But if you helped us—"

"I don't really have…" Slowly, he turned to face Willie. He blinked, rubbed his eyes, then continued to stare.

"Uh, Holden." The other young woman tried to get his attention.

He turned back to them. "Next week. If you don't mind, I have something urgent to deal with. Be safe on the way home."

"We were hoping you could walk us—"

"Just go, please. You've walked home every night after class and been fine."

"But we might not be—"

"I have to go." Holden grabbed his backpack, slung it over his shoulder, and headed toward the door. He snagged Willie's elbow and brought him along for the ride.

Amused, I followed.

Holden aimed Willie into an alcove. "You're wearing clothes."

"Yes."

"I can touch you."

"Yes."

Holden gave Willie the once-over, ending on his nose. "That looks painful."

"I might've walked into a wall. Uh, after I…" He glanced at me, then back at Holden. "Rematerialized."

After holding Willie's gaze for a long moment, Holden glanced in my direction. He gazed directly into my eyes, but clearly, he didn't see me.

Disappointment swamped me. Why I'd thought things might've changed was beyond me. And I'd watched Juliette leave this afternoon. At least Willie could still see me.

"Who's here?" Holden turned back to Willie.

"Duncan."

"The Civil War soldier?"

Willie nodded.

Holden waved in my direction. "Hi."

"He says *hi* back." Willie glanced my way, daring me to argue. He turned back to Holden. "He's a good guy."

"You've said."

Okay, well, that piqued my curiosity.

"Willie." I injected a sharp note to help focus the flustered man.

"Yeah."

"We need to get you out of here. If we *can…*" Holden frowned.

That apparently stopped all three of us as we held ourselves still.

Holden tilted his head. "Have you ever tried to leave the school grounds?"

Willie shook his head. "No. I just…knew I couldn't… Does that make sense?"

"I've tried."

My friend shot his gaze to me.

Holden did as well, although the confusion written across his face made it clear he was merely following Willie's lead.

"You've tried?" Willie held my gaze.

"Yes. It…didn't end well. For some reason, I cannot

leave. I imagine, however, now that you're corporeal, you should be able to leave."

"But you don't know for certain."

"William—"

He glared.

I continued. "I believe you have nothing to lose. If you're able to leave, then go. If you stay, someone who was around back in 1989 might recognize you. The principal, right? She was a teacher and now an administrator."

"Yeah…I knew her."

"Then you need to go."

He appeared stricken. "I don't want to leave you."

My heart broke a little because I wouldn't want to leave him either. "You have no reason to stay, William." I specifically used his full name. Not just because I was well aware it irritated him—but also to put distance between the two of us. To show I had no emotional connection to him.

All the while knowing that to be a lie.

"Right." He blinked a couple of times. "Of course." He turned back to Holden. "Can I come home with you?"

He winced. "My place is pretty small." Then he appeared to ponder. "We'll work something out. Let's go." He snagged Willie by the elbow and nearly propelled him out the door.

Willie looked back over his shoulder.

I waved.

He left.

I staggered. I hadn't realized…hadn't known I would feel this way. In some ways, we'd known each other—known of each other—for decades. In some ways, though, we'd only just started to form a true relationship. I'd thought maybe we might form…a bond? Did ghosts fall in love? Did I have the right to see what we'd shared that way? Because this parting felt far worse than anything I'd expected. I'd seen other ghosts leave, but I'd never felt bereft at their leaving. More happy for them. They'd moved on. I never would.

Now, though? With Willie walking out of my life forever?

My heart truly shattered.

Chapter Fifteen

Oliver

I should've known something was wrong when I found myself alone in the locker room with Larry, Dominic, and Gary.

I hadn't, of course. Instead, I'd been all in my head thinking about Holden and when I'd see him next. I hated that we were only in Spanish together. Well, and a shared shift at the grocery store. But those were times when we couldn't be alone. I considered him a friend, of a sort, but I hadn't found the courage to tell him that.

Or anything else.

Instead, I casually approached him every chance I got. At least when it wouldn't be obvious I was seeking him out. Which meant usually Juliette or Peyton was around. And I didn't mind, because they were really nice young women. Most of the people in this high school were friendly. The dark voice in my mind wondered if that friendliness was just because I was a good kicker or because everyone was genuine.

Again, no clue.

"Well, if it isn't the nephew." Larry glared.

I sought a quick exit, only to have it blocked by the other two shitheads. All three were meatheads. Over the past month, I'd tried to find redeeming qualities in any of the three.

Nope, not a single one. Instead, I'd witnessed them bullying smaller kids. Berating girls they perceived as *ugly*. I kept hoping a teacher or Principal Kouriki would notice, but they never seemed to.

If you don't speak out, how would they know? You should've said something a long time ago. The time for regrets was over. I grabbed my backpack. Unfortunately, Uncle Jeremiah wasn't able to pick me up tonight—he had something in Chapel Hill. Aunt Leslie was at her book club—which she treasured. She'd offered to skip, but I'd assured her I could get home on my own.

In other words, no one waited for me at the front of the school and who might come to my rescue. "If you don't mind." I tried to get through without actually touching anyone.

Dominic smacked his shoulder against mine, sending me back a few steps.

"Guys." I put on my most charming smile. "My aunt's waiting for me."

"Your White aunt." Gary sneered.

My hackles rose. "My mother's sister. My dead mother's sister. I think I've got enough grief, don't you?" I didn't use the orphan card often, but now felt like a suitable moment. Any ploy for sympathy that might work was worth trying.

All three appeared completely unmoved.

Sorry, Mom.

"Look, guys, I'm not sure what we're doing here." Because playing dumb rarely worked, but I was willing. "Coach Pinker wanted to see me—"

"Coach Pinker left for the day." Dominic sneered. "No one here to save you."

Panic encroached, but I knocked it back with the

baseball bat I wished I had. "What are you going to do? Beat me up? So badly that I'm injured—leaving you without a kicker. Do you honestly believe I won't say anything? That I'll either quit school—leaving you without a kicker—or say nothing and wait for you to do it again? You're bullies. Bullies never stop. So I suggest you just walk out, and we can forget this ever happened." *And I'll find a way to let administration know what's going on. I'm not going to cower anymore.* If they were clearly willing to hurt me, what would they do to others if left to their own devices? *This has to stop.*

Gary grabbed one arm while Larry reached for the other. I swung wildly, but he sidestepped, nabbing my arm as I brought it back. I snarled even as he held me.

Again, panic settled low in my gut. I wasn't a big muscular guy like Dominic. And although Larry played basketball, he had a solid grip. Apparently, lacrosse players were strong as well, because Gary had a firm grip. If I tried to fight at this point, we were all going to get hurt—me most of all.

Dominic balled his fist and aimed for my midsection.

I tried to tighten my abs, thinking I'd heard something about that lessening damage.

The locker door banged open.

Gary and Larry dropped my arms.

Instinctively, I yanked those arms close to my body. They weren't getting a grasp again without serious effort.

Dominic smoothly raised his hand and scratched his scalp.

Hank pushed his mop and bucket on wheels into the room. He gazed up at us. "Oh, I was sure you boys had left." He made a show of looking at his watch. "Best you head out now. Homework and all."

Gary grunted. But he was also the first to grab his bag and boot out of there.

Dominic appeared to rethink his options before he also took off.

Larry remained where he was. "We're just talking. Why don't you leave us alone, old man? This is none of your business."

Hank straightened, slowly taking his mop into his hands in what could only be described as a fighter's stance. "I wouldn't disrespect your elders, Mr. Arnold."

My nemesis appeared momentarily taken aback that Hank knew his name. I doubted he knew the janitor's. I'd taken the time, early on, to learn all the faculty and staff's names.

"Hello, Hank." *Should've learned his last name— that would've shown him the respect he deserves. Still…work with what you have.*

"Nice to see you, Mr. Barton. How are you finding school these days? I understand we won the game on Friday night because of a field goal you kicked." He eyed Larry. "Would be a shame if anything happened to our star kicker."

"I'm out of here." Larry grabbed his gym bag, brushed past Hank, and nearly ran as he took off.

For the first time in about ten minutes, I took in a lungful of air. I didn't even mind the funky smell.

I met Hank's gaze. "Thank you."

He shrugged. "I didn't do anything. But did I see something?"

For the longest of moments, I considered. Guilt over not speaking up earlier won over cowardice. "I'll talk to

Principal Kouriki in the morning."

"Mention my name." He dunked his mop in the bucket. Then he met my gaze. "I'll back you up." He shook his head. "They're…not good kids. I try to believe everyone is redeemable, but I've seen a few kids over the years who are just black in their souls. I don't know if any of those three can be saved. But maybe, with your help, they can be forced to take responsibility." He winked. "I think Gary will cave. He's got a scholarship to a university up north as a lacrosse player. He won't want to lose it."

"You think he'll see the light?" I wasn't convinced.

Hank appeared to contemplate my question. "Some people can change. You have." He wrung out his mop, then placed it on the floor.

I cocked my head. "How?"

"You're…coming into your own. You're seeing people for who they are. You're…making good friends."

"Holden." I whispered his name.

He winked. "You'll do okay. You should get going. Keep your phone close in case anything happens. We didn't have those in my day."

Which made me wonder what *his day* was. My mom had enjoyed explaining to me that not everyone had grown up with a cell phone attached to their hand or a computer in their house.

I couldn't fathom.

As I passed Hank, I held out my hand to shake.

He met my gaze, then shook my hand.

I swallowed. "Thank you. I don't know how you knew…" Because I didn't believe, even for a second, that he'd *just happened* to have wandered in here.

"A friend…" He cleared his throat. "A friend

suggested you might be in trouble. I got here as soon as I could."

"In the nick of time." An expression that I'd never really understood until this moment. "Thank you."

"My pleasure. You head on home."

"Yeah." I squeezed, then let him go. I probably shouldn't have touched him, but I needed that connection. To ground me. To reassure him that I was okay. To reassure myself that I would be okay.

I headed out of the locker room and down the hall. I tried not to jump at every noise as several groups had activities tonight, including the theater group. Part of me wished I had a talent for being someone else. Maybe I could walk away from my life for a night and inhabit another person's life.

As I passed Principal Kouriki's door, I caught sight of a light through the crack. I'd told Hank—virtually promised him—that I'd speak to her in the morning.

Why wait?

I knocked on the door.

After a long moment, she opened it. She blinked several times, as if trying to place me. With so many students, I didn't blame her. Then she smiled. "Mr. Barton. To what do I owe the pleasure?"

"Do you have a moment?"

"Of course. Let me just let Mr. Copeland, the school counselor, know you're here."

At first, I didn't understand. Then I did. She needed someone to know she would be alone with a student. I was grateful she understood I didn't want to share this with anyone while appreciating her prudence.

After a moment, she gestured me in. "How can I help?"

Chapter Sixteen

Peyton

"Okay." I gazed at Juliette. "You understand monomial?"

Slowly, she nodded.

"Okay, well, polynomials are…just a bit more complicated."

She groaned. "I think polyamory is less complicated."

I burst out laughing. "Really? Managing a relationship with two other people? I can barely keep myself together, let alone factoring for a second and a third."

"I think you'd be good in either a couple or a triad." She twirled her pencil. "You're very kind. Very sensitive. Very in tune with what others need."

Although I didn't believe a single word coming from her, I was also intrigued where she was going with this. She couldn't know how I felt about her, of course. I'd been the perfect math tutor over the past month. And as much as she tried, she was not the model student. She wanted to spend all our time together teaching me about biology. I wanted derivatives and quadratics.

Neither of us was making much progress. I might understand cell biology…sort of…but genetics tripped me up every time. All I wanted to do was talk about DNA databases. Like…if I submitted my DNA and they discovered my cousin Irving was really a serial killer, would I feel badly he got caught?

In a word? No. Bully could rot in jail for all I cared.

"Sensitive?" I had to get us back on track. "I don't think that's a concept in calculus."

"But it could be a trait in biology." She tried to move our math textbooks out of the way.

Gently, I pushed them back. "We said calc tonight and bio tomorrow." Technically, I should've been helping Holden tonight. But Juliette had a big test on Friday and was totally not ready.

She huffed.

I grinned.

A knock sounded at my back door. A special knock I knew well. The knock was louder than I would've liked, but my parents were out, so not such a big deal. I hopped up and made my way to the door.

The knock came again.

I hustled faster. "I'm coming. Good grief, keep your pants on…" I opened the door half a foot. I sighed dramatically. "Holden."

His hair was disheveled. As if he'd run his hand through it a bunch of times. He met my gaze, his eyes a little wild. "Yeah, can we come in?"

For just a moment, I didn't understand the question. Then I spotted the guy standing just behind him. A kid I'd never seen before. "Sure…" I opened the door farther.

Holden coaxed the guy inside.

Juliette, clearly having decided this was more interesting than calculus, came into the kitchen. She grinned. "Holden, it's so great you're here."

He blinked. "Oh. Calculus not going well?"

She shivered dramatically.

They both laughed.

I gestured to the new guy. "And you are…"

"Uh, Willie."

"Great. Lovely to meet you. You're a friend of Holden's?" I gave my best friend a look that said, *we're talking about this later*.

Willie managed a smile. Clearly an effort. "Yes, I am. I…" He winced. "May I use your facilities?"

"My bathroom?"

He nodded.

"Sure."

"I'll show you." Juliette nodded over her shoulder. "There are a bunch of doors in this house."

Not that many, but clearly she saw I needed a moment alone with Holden. When the two departed, I turned to him. "What's really going on?"

"You have to fucking help us."

"Juliette's here." I might've whisper-hissed that.

His expression dripped sarcasm as he rolled his eyes. "This is more important." Then he bit his lip. "Mom's not working tonight. Her night off. So bringing Willie home didn't make sense. I mean, we've only got three bedrooms."

"I'm assuming he needs a place to crash for the night?"

He nodded.

"You couldn't, I don't know, share?" I pretended to glance over at the direction of the bathroom. "He's not exactly your type—"

"He's a friend." Holden bit that off.

"One you've never mentioned." I countered a little

more snippily than I intended. Holden was a big boy. He was allowed to have friends. Still, a little hurt crept in. I told him everything. Clearly, he had a secret.

He glared. "It's not like that."

"Oh?"

"Willie…" He glanced over his shoulder. "He's different."

"Well, yeah."

"Huh?"

"Very few people can pull off that haircut, Holden. Hello?" I mimicked holding up a phone. "The eighties are calling, and they want their *do* back." I grinned. "My dad used to have hair like that." I shivered. Then eyed him. "How is it you never mentioned him?"

"You don't have to be sarcastic." He glared. "It's not cool. Just because you're not getting any—"

"Shush." I hissed the word at him.

"Too close to the truth?" He grinned.

"We're talking about *your* friend. Who will be back any moment."

"Okay." He winced. "I need you to just believe me."

Clearly, he was serious, so I sobered a bit. "What?"

"Yes, Holden, what's going on?" Juliette's voice rang clear.

Props for not even pretending you haven't been eavesdropping. Sometimes she had way more guts than I did.

Holden took a deep breath, and for the next five minutes, I just stood in shock as he explained about some ghost he'd met in the school library. How that ghost had just come to life. How that ghost was in my bathroom.

At some point, I held up my hand. "Okay." I took a breath. "I'm trying to find a way not to call for some *help* for you."

Even as I said the words, though, Juliette blurted out, "Oh, what about Duncan? Did he come to life?"

"Willie's Duncan?" Holden tilted his head.

She frowned. "I always thought of him as Duncan's Willie." She scrunched her nose. "Yeah, that doesn't work."

Under any other circumstances, I would've commented. But tonight required decorum and—

Nope, had to do it. "Duncan's willy? Really? Is that what we call peckers these days?" I burst out laughing. Right…better than to admit my best friend and the girl I had a massive crush on both saw ghosts. "Willie's Duncan? That's the ghost you can see, right?"

"What about Duncan's willy?" The ghost, painfully named Willie, reappeared. He met my gaze. "You have a cheerful house. Reminds me of mine."

My house, although lovely, was firmly decorated almost a half century ago. My mother had inherited it from her parents when they moved to Boca Raton, and she'd insisted everything remain the same. I wasn't convinced my father enjoyed the shrine to his in-laws, but I also figured that he liked being mortgage free more, so he'd held his tongue. "Uh, thank you. My mother would enjoy the compliment."

"Where is Duncan?" Juliette waved around as if trying to conjure something. Or, apparently, someone.

"He didn't…that is…"

"You left him alone?" She headed toward the front door. "I have to go see him."

I tried to head her off. "It's night. No one's left at school. You're saying…" I glanced over my shoulder at Willie.

As if understanding my question, he nodded.

I turned back to Juliette. "Okay, so your friend's a ghost. Duncan?"

She spun and headed to my bedroom with Willie and I hard on her heels. She started stuffing all her study materials into her backpack. "Yes." She held my gaze. "I didn't imagine him."

"Oh, she totally didn't." Holden strolled in. He turned to Juliette. "How long?"

"Since the beginning of school this year. He just appeared while I was studying, and…" She shrugged. "I've always believed in spirits. I figured that's why he chose me. But he said in one hundred and sixty years, he's never been seen before."

This time, I waved my hand. "Duncan is one hundred and sixty years old?"

Willie slowly raised his hand. "Technically, he's one eighty. He was twenty when he died."

"Of course he was." I wanted to tell them they were all batshit…but I believed them. All of them. If anything, Willie's haircut sealed the deal. I pivoted to Holden. "And when could you first see…him?" I indicated the interloper.

"Well…" Holden flushed.

"I was naked." Willie volunteered that information with very little encouragement.

I arched an eyebrow at my best friend. "You've been able to see a naked ghost since—"

"First day of school."

"—the first day of school, and you never thought to mention this?"

Willie held up his hand again. "I asked him not to."

I turned my annoyance on him. "Is that the truth?"

"Well…no…"

"Then why lie to me?"

"Because—" Willie wiped his brow. "—you're mad at my friend. I haven't had a lot of friends."

I cocked my head.

Juliette grasped his hand. "You have friends now, Willie. And I think Duncan's your friend."

"Oh." He blinked. "Well, I meant from before. In high school I didn't have friends. Just people who made fun of me."

"That's horrible." She continued to grasp his hand. "We're your friends."

"Wow." He sniffed. "That's really sweet."

Part of me wanted to roll my eyes, and part of me wanted to give the kid a hug. Painfully thin, clearly awkward, and with thick lenses in his glasses, he did look a little dorky. The haircut was *not* helping. "You're hoping to stay here?" I eyed Holden. "My parents might be clueless about a lot of things, but I think they'll notice *him.*"

"We have to help Duncan." Juliette stomped.

Actually stomped.

Which, admittedly, didn't have the effect she undoubtedly wanted. Barefoot. Shag carpet. Barely a whisper.

Still adorable.

Holden's phone buzzed with an incoming text. He snatched it from his back pocket, read the text, and frowned.

"What?" I might've snapped that. I was trying to absorb the fact my best friend and my crush could both see ghosts and hadn't told me. Basically, I was trying not to feel hurt.

"Oliver's at school. He said he knows it's late but was wondering if I wanted to meet up."

"Like meet up, meet up or *meet up*, meet up?"

He held up the screen. "You think you can divine greater meaning from his words, have at it."

"You don't have to be snippy."

Juliette held up her hand. "Why don't we all just head over to Pinedale High? Then we can check on Duncan and meet Oliver."

I wasn't entirely certain why we needed to check up on a man who'd been dead more than a sesquicentennial, but clearly we weren't going to get to more integers this evening. Or further delve into why Juliette found me *sensitive* and how that wasn't a bad thing. And yeah, I was pretty proud of myself for knowing the term for one hundred and fifty years. Something had passed that mark recently in Raleigh, and I'd liked the word.

"Are we all going?" Juliette eyed me.

"Yeah, I'm in." I glanced at Willie. "You'll need a coat. I think my sister left something behind that will fit you. Kind of butch." I glared at Holden, thinking back to our conversation all those weeks ago.

"Nothing wrong with butch," he affirmed.

"Nothing at all," Juliette added.

I met her gaze, trying to figure out if she was sending me some kind of message or was just generally commenting.

Naturally, I couldn't tell.

Five minutes later, we headed over to Pinedale High.

Chapter Seventeen

Juliette

I wanted to hustle, but Willie and Peyton had begun a protracted discussion about eighties movies. Normally, I enjoyed my friend's quirkiness. Today, I wished we could just hurry along.

"So you know Duncan?" Holden kept glancing at Willie.

I couldn't get a read on their relationship. I just read friendship, but I was crap at things like that. Couples would announce they were together, and everyone would say how they'd seen it coming, and I would be like…*huh? Them? And everyone knew…how?* Sometimes I felt like I lived in a bubble of ignorance.

And I was the head cheerleader, for Pete's sake. I frowned. Another of my mom's quaint expressions that none of my friends used. I had to be careful not to speak them aloud. "Yeah, I know Duncan. I just…" I shrugged. "Maybe I should've been more concerned, but he was just there. In his Civil War uniform. And I figured he was pretty innocuous. Couldn't help me with calculus but had great stories."

"To help you procrastinate." He laughed.

"Not that I needed help."

"No, but if you'd mastered the subject, you wouldn't need Peyton's help."

I nearly tripped. "I suppose." *How are we not closer to the school?*

He grinned as he continued walking. "So, Duncan…"

"Not sure what you're asking. He's…challenging. He doesn't like talking much. About anything. I've learned a few things about him. Would love to know more, but that's not likely."

"Why do you say that?"

"He's not…verbose. He's not…chatty."

"Unlike Peyton."

I snickered. "That's true."

We rounded the corner as the school came into sight. In a text exchange, Oliver agreed to hang by one of the side doors. We shouldn't have been going *into* the school at nearly eight o'clock—and would probably catch heck if an adult found us. Still, despite the risk, I felt we needed to get to Duncan. Finding him and making certain he was okay seemed super important at the moment. Like something I had to do *right* now.

Holden waved as Oliver stuck his head out.

We all picked up the pace.

A quick glance assured me no cars remained in the parking lot. But with Pinedale being so small and with so many houses nearby, many teachers and staff walked.

Oliver glanced around. "The principal was going to drive me home, but I told her I'd wait for Uncle Jeremiah, only I realized he's going to be late tonight. Everyone else is gone, I think."

Holden ducked in first while Oliver held the door for the rest of us.

"Anyone see you?" Holden glanced around. Although I'd been the one to insist we come down, he seemed to be the one in charge. Or taking charge. Or something.

Watch. Peyton's not going to let him get away with that for long.

As if on cue, she turned to me. "Where do you normally see Duncan?"

"Mrs. Bletchley's room."

She turned to Willie. "And you?"

He pressed a hand to his chest. "Pretty much everywhere."

She turned to Oliver. "This is Willie. He used to be a ghost."

Oliver's soft blue eyes widened. "Uh, care to repeat that?"

Holden waved him off. "We have to find Willie's friend first." He cast a quick glance at me. "We're worried about him."

"Oh…okay." Oliver tightened his grip on his backpack. "If you say so."

"He does." Peyton snagged Willie's elbow. "Let's try Mrs. Bletchley's classroom first. If he's not there…we'll just check everywhere."

"Right. Shouldn't we consider splitting up?" Oliver hustled—along with the rest of us—to keep up with Peyton. For a shorter person, she sure knew how to hurry.

"Only Willie and Juliette can see Duncan." Holden offered this up helpfully. "So we could—"

"We stick together." Peyton halted us. She checked the hallway before we all turned and headed down it.

"How late does Hank work?" Oliver whispered the question to no one in particular.

"Not unreasonably so," Willie offered. "I mean, it

feels like he's always here."

"The omnipresent janitor." Holden said that with a touch of sarcasm, then winced. "Sorry, not funny."

"Oh, I think Hank might think it is." Willie grinned. "He's got a good sense of humor. I mean, what little I know of him—"

"Hush." Peyton hissed that. "The entire building will be able to hear all of you."

"Well, most won't care." Willie ran his hand through his hair. "They ignore the humans."

She stopped abruptly.

I nearly knocked into her, stopping at the last second. "What the heck, Peyton?"

She spun Willie to face her. "Exactly *how many* ghosts are there?"

"Uh…" He pulled his lower lip through his teeth, then scrunched his nose. "I probably shouldn't say."

She glared.

I would've been cowed.

Then she wielded that glare on me.

Yep, cowed. She was just…fire. I held up my hands. "I only ever saw Duncan."

She pivoted to Holden.

"Don't ask me—Naked Kid's been the only one."

We all turned to Willie who blushed beet red.

"It's a long story. I think you said Mrs. Bletchley's class…"

Okay, well, I definitely wanted to hear that story.

We arrived at Mrs. Bletchley's door. For a moment, we all stood there.

Then Holden sucked in an audible breath. "Don't they usually lock the classroom doors at night?"

Oliver shrugged. "I think so…"

"We're not going to know if we don't try." I shouldered everyone out of the way and tried the knob.

It opened.

"See? Such wimps." I pushed my way into the dark classroom.

Peyton flipped on the light.

A chorus of, *heys* and *what the fucks* rang out from the others.

She held up her hand to silence all of us. "Can you see ghosts in the dark?"

"Uh, that's the whole point. They're…ghostly. White, like." Holden hesitated as he looked at Willie. "Right?"

She snickered. "Now you're thinking of asking—"

"Hi, Duncan." I offered a little wave.

Everyone spun in the direction I waved.

"Holy shit." Oliver whispered the words. "Is he wearing—"

"Yes."

"And he's—"

"Yes."

Oliver straightened. "Well, okay then. Uh, nice to meet you." He pivoted to Willie. "Nice to meet you too. You used to be a ghost?"

"Keep up, cutie." Peyton pivoted from Oliver and indicated Duncan. "Why can we all see you?"

Duncan cocked his head.

"I don't know, but something's changing," I explained.

"You are…correct." His gaze flitted from me to Willie. "Back so soon? I'd have thought you'd be finished with us."

Willie gestured to me. "She said we had to come. I

figured the risk of becoming a ghost again was pretty slim." He looked around. "That having been said, I'd like shoes with better treads, and I don't want to be anywhere near wet floors."

Huh? Something else we'd figure out at a later point. I met Duncan's stare. "Are you okay?"

"I am." He shrugged. "No different from any other night."

"Right." I nodded. "But he—" I sought the right word. "—rematerialized tonight. So, like, you might do the same too, huh?"

"I do not believe so. I am still unclear why William is now back in the land of the living. So to speak."

Willie groaned. "Please don't call me that."

"That was his father's name," Holden offered as an explanation. "He honestly prefers Willie."

Duncan looked as if he was contemplating, a little furrow appearing in his brow. "He never told me that."

Holden shrugged. "I get the feeling there are quite a few things he's never shared." He turned to Willie.

Who blushed again. "Uh…" He took a deep breath. "I died when I slipped in the shower and fell. I slipped because Frank Fletcher came in and I didn't want him to see how attracted I was to him."

I was still really confused.

"And it turns out Frank is a really horrible person." He straightened. "I, uh, came out."

Still confused.

Holden clapped Willie on the back.

Willie startled, glancing over at Holden. He was clearly surprised at being touched, let alone smacked playfully.

"I bet you did what you needed to do—found a way

to be true to yourself." Holden turned to Duncan. "We just need to figure out what you need to do, and maybe you can rematerialize as well."

"What if he doesn't want to?" To my surprise, I spoke up. "Not everyone wants to live this life. He has eternity. What if he isn't ready to give that up?"

Willie slowly raised his hand. "I honestly hadn't thought of that. I just accepted I told my truth that I'd been holding back for so long, and I realized I wasn't scared to be me anymore. I wasn't a bad person—my death wasn't my fault. It was like this heavy weight lifting off me, and then, poof, I was human again." He touched his cheeks almost reverentially. Like he couldn't believe he was real.

"Yeah, I hope so too. We have better treatments for acne now." Holden slung an arm around Willie. "I'll take care of you."

Oliver's mouth drooped.

Peyton snickered. "While he lives at my place in Lily's old room? You know, eventually, my parents are going to notice. Eventually, we'll have to explain this to, I dunno, an adult."

"Duncan first." I indicated everyone should sit. "If he wants to. We figure out why he hasn't rematerialized, and then we can…tell someone." I didn't have the first clue what would be involved. I couldn't even contemplate how we'd go about it. Tell the truth and look crazy? Try to figure out a cover story? Like what? At the very least Willie's haircut had to go. Maybe we could claim we found him on the side of the road and he didn't remember who he was?

That had possibilities.

I sat. "Okay, Duncan. What truth haven't you

accepted?"

He cleared his throat.

Which was weird for a ghost, but whatever.

"I…" He plopped down on a chair across from all of us. "There are things you don't know about me."

"Does this have to do with your wife? Or the man you loved?" Willie nearly vibrated in his seat. "Because you admitted all that to me already."

"You're…bisexual?" I met Duncan's gaze. "I have to say I didn't see that coming. You said you'd never been attracted to someone."

He crossed his legs. "I lied to you. I apologize. I didn't know you very well at first, and by the time I did…the time had passed for intimate revelations." He scanned the group. "We didn't have a term for it. I knew homosexuality was a sin. And would most likely end in death if I was exposed. My friend…" He cleared his throat again. "My friends were lovers, and they both died in the second battle of Fort Wagner." He gazed out the window, into the inky darkness.

Nothing to see. Unless there are other ghosts. With that distant look, I imagined he wasn't really seeing the night outside.

"We succeeded finally at the Battle of Boykin's Mill. The Massachusetts 54th took huge losses…but we won the battle, and in the end, we won the war."

Oliver spoke first. "That's good, right?"

"A small group of us wanted to come home right away." He scratched his chin. "I had a wife at home who had written about another man. I didn't want to wait till I got discharged. A small group of us left the army one night and headed north from South Carolina. Then we were set upon, unexpectedly." His jaw tightened. "We might've been deserters, but we didn't deserve the undignified deaths we had."

Slowly, I pointed to the floor.

He nodded. "The three of us are buried out near the football field. Our graves were never discovered."

"Oh." Willie pressed a hand to his mouth.

"Did the other two become ghosts?"

Duncan shook his head. "Not that I know. I awoke lying on the ground, and…" He appeared to consider. "I knew I was dead. No question. I wasn't cold. Wasn't hot. Just…wasn't. Eventually, I stood, but when I tried to walk farther than about one hundred feet, I started to disappear. Obviously, I came back. I do not know why my compatriots did not become ghosts. Well, I saw someone die here and haven't ever seen their ghost, so I believe it doesn't happen to everyone." He appeared to wave off that notion. "I've kept Mary, Fiona, and all the others company over these many years."

"Mary? Fiona?" Peyton cocked her head. "All of the others?"

"Yes. Mary was here long before me. She was escaping the Salem Witch Trials. She wasn't a witch, but she was accused of being one. She headed south, hoping to reach family in Charleston. Instead of making it, she died just a few feet from where I lay. Some natives found her body and gave her a burial. She also is hemmed in by some kind of containment." He scratched his chin again. "The castle was built and then destroyed. Fiona was part of that mess. Those are the ruins they discovered when they started the renovations. There are Indigenous spirits as well. Lots and lots and lots of ghosts."

"And the school?" I was curious and wanted to know. More importantly, I wanted Duncan to come back to life.

He nodded. "When the town, and eventually the school, were built, our boundaries became clear. The school and surrounding grounds, but no farther. The first school building burned down about seventy years ago. We all sat on the football field and watched it happen. And then the town rebuilt it."

"And you still couldn't leave." I tapped my finger on the desk. "So what do you have to discover? Or say? Or do?"

"Would this have something to do with your body?" Holden pursed his lips. "Like, if your body's recovered and given a proper burial, would that make a difference?"

"Or maybe just recording the details of your death." Peyton squinted in that cute way she did when she was thinking really hard. "You would've been reported as a deserter. So your family never knew what happened to you."

"Well, they're all long dead now, so that doesn't likely matter to anyone." Holden sounded just a little snippy.

"Are we keeping you up past your bedtime?" I winked at him.

He blew out a long breath. "Why don't we figure this out? Who has a laptop or tablet?"

"I do." I yanked my netbook out of my bag. I'd been working on my English assignment before hooking up with Peyton to do math. "Okay, what am I looking for?"

"Well…" Holden nodded to our ghost. "What's your full name and rank?"

Duncan straightened. "Corporal Duncan Jeremiah Galloway of the Massachusetts 54th."

Oliver gasped. "Oh my God."

We all turned our attention to him.

All color drained from his face.

"Hey, are you going to pass out?" I grabbed his hand since I was close.

Holden was even closer, and he crouched over Oliver. "What's wrong? You need to talk to us."

"My uncle." He cleared his throat. "My uncle is Jeremiah John Galloway. Named after a distant relative."

A heavy silence hung in the room.

"We wouldn't be…" Duncan gestured between Oliver and himself. "Are you saying…"

"My uncle is Black. And…" Oliver gently nudged Holden to the side to stare intently at Duncan. "And you really look like him."

I pointed to my netbook. "I think we've got some work to do."

For the next two hours, we traced the genealogy of Duncan and the two other men who'd accompanied him. Why I hadn't done this earlier, I wasn't certain. He was such a private man. Holding himself in a stiff and formal manner. Only three years older than me but so very many more in lived experience.

By the end, not only had we found definitive proof that Duncan was related to Oliver's uncle, but we'd traced the families of the other two men.

I shut my netbook and eyed Duncan. "I think you need time to process this. Do we ask for excavation? Which, I admit, is a tough sell. Do we contact the other two families to let them know about their loved ones? According to records, both were presumed lost at Boykin's Mill in that battle. Do we want their relatives to know they were actually…"

"Deserters," he prompted.

"Deserters," I echoed. "You were presumed a deserter." I eyed Oliver. "How did that affect your uncle's family?"

He scratched his light stubble.

The time inched closer to midnight.

"I don't honestly know. We've never spoken about his family. Which, I suppose, might be a clue. But I only know three generations back from my mother's and father's families. I didn't ask them questions when they were alive, and when my grandmother tried to talk about the family—all of whom were dead—I shut her down. Losing my parents was still too raw. It never occurred to me that I might later want to know about them. That I might regret not listening." He winced. "I regret it now."

"You've got your aunt, though, right?" Holden patted Oliver on the back. "She could tell you about your mom's family. Maybe even your dad's…if you asked her."

"I suppose." His blue eyes shone. "It's a big ask. She lost her sister as well that horrible day my parents died."

"But she didn't lose you." Holden crouched before Oliver, gazing up into his eyes. "It doesn't have to be today…or even tomorrow." He offered a wry smile. "I think sharing Duncan's existence will be enough of a shock for one day." He glanced over his shoulder. "If you're okay with us sharing."

Duncan grabbed the ends of his military jacket and yanked. As if trying to find the courage to face what lay ahead.

The jacket creaked.

Everyone held very still.

At first, I didn't think Duncan realized what

167

happened.

Holden rose, moving aside. Oliver and Duncan stared at each other—undoubtedly with the same disbelief the rest of us had.

"Can you stand?" Oliver spoke first.

Duncan scowled. "Of course I can stand."

He did.

And nearly knocked the desk over.

We all rushed over to him.

Willie got there first, supporting Duncan by the elbow. "I felt super woozy at first. You have to, well, breathe. And eventually, you'll really need to pee."

I tittered. As did just about everyone else.

To his credit, Willie didn't falter. "At least you're dressed. I mean, imagine me. I wasn't even dressed. And I wasn't surrounded by people. I was by myself, which was good, I suppose, since I was, you know, naked."

The classroom door swung open.

I held my breath. Until Hank the janitor entered.

He took us all in. "What's going on?" He surveyed us all, but settled on Willie and Duncan. "Oh." He nodded to Willie. "You're okay?"

Willie nodded back.

"I am too." Duncan stood a little straighter. But didn't shake off Willie's supporting hand. "I… Things are different."

"Truly." Hank waved his hand around. "Can you leave the grounds?"

Willie continued to nod like a bobblehead. "I can. I assume Duncan can. It's so cool. Oh, Hank, you have no idea."

The older man smiled. "I think I do." Then he sobered. "You have to leave. You can't stay all night. I should've been gone a while ago, but…" He shrugged. "I got involved in something."

He sees ghosts too. My gut told me that I should question this closer. *Later*. Something, some instinct, was pushing at me. Being on the grounds at midnight felt like a really bad idea. "Hank's right—we need to leave. Peyton, do you have a room for both Willie and Duncan?"

She shook her head. "I might've been able to sneak in one scrawny White kid—"

"Hey." Willie's protest contained a bit of a whine.

Duncan placed his hand over Willie's. "Let her speak."

Willie set his mouth in a mutinous line but held his tongue.

"No way I can take them home." Holden winced. "Our place is way too small."

Oliver raised his hand. "We have a basement. I don't think my aunt and uncle go down there. Not during the week, at least. So there's a pull-out couch, if you two don't mind sharing a bed."

"A bed?" Duncan whispered the word reverently. "I haven't lain on a bed since 1863."

Willie giggled. "Only 1989 for me. Sleep…" He gazed at Duncan. "Do we need sleep?"

As if on cue, Duncan, Holden, and I yawned. When I suppressed it—and my ears popped—I grinned. "Okay, homeward bound." I turned to Hank. "Thank you." I assumed that he wasn't going to say anything. That he'd keep our secret.

He met everyone's gaze, finally settling his intense stare on the former ghosts. "Make good choices. Live good lives." With that, he departed.

I shook my head to clear my thoughts. "Okay, we need to have a really long conversation with him in the daylight, because clearly he knows a lot more than he's telling."

Willie and Duncan exchanged a look I couldn't interpret.

Okay...or maybe not.

We gathered our backpacks. Oliver and I lived pretty close, with Peyton and Holden on the other side of town. We said our goodbyes and split up. I gestured to Holden to make certain Peyton got home safe. They lived close, but I needed to be certain he'd look after her.

Behind her back, he gave me the thumbs-up.

As if by agreement, we walked in silence until we got to my house. On impulse, I hugged all three guys. Somehow, tonight, we'd bonded. The six of us would never be the same. Of that, I was certain.

I snuck in the side door and was halfway to the stairs when my mother spoke.

"Juliette."

"Uh, hi, Mom." I tried for a casual smile. "Sorry. Lost track of time."

"It's that girl. The one with the purple hair. She's a bad influence on you."

I took a deep breath. "Mom, Peyton's my friend. I know she has purple hair. But she offered to hit a guy with her clarinet because he's a racist asshole. I like her—"

"Language, Juliette."

I stuck out my chin. "I apologize for the asshole comment."

She winced.

"But I won't apologize for my amazing friend. She's

changed my life. And not just with calculus class. I'm…happier, Mom. Like my life has purpose."

"Your life always had purpose, my child." Her eyes shimmered. "I'm sorry you ever doubted that."

"There's more."

She arched an eyebrow.

"I need you to write me a note to get out of school tomorrow. And…" I took a deep breath. "And not ask any questions."

For a long moment, she held my gaze. "I need a bit more than that."

This is going to be an awkward conversation.

But I loved my mom, so I laid it all on the line. My feelings for Peyton. How I didn't want to be a doctor. How I had friends who needed my help.

She called the school to leave an absence voicemail telling them I wouldn't be there the next day.

She gave me a big hug.

She told me she loved me.

One hurdle cleared. We'll see what tomorrow brings.

Chapter Eighteen

Willie

Despite being exhausted, I couldn't sleep.

Duncan had no such problem. His head hit the pillow, and within moments, he slept. Profoundly. His deep, even breaths lulled me…but only so much.

Had he been tired when he died? Was that the reason? Or was I awake because I couldn't believe I was alive? In a bed. With a man I now saw very differently. For years, I didn't dare go near him. He was a soldier. He gave the impression he didn't want to be approached. I'd seen him with Mary, Fiona, and a few others, but that hadn't given me the courage to seek him out.

Given how lonely I'd been, I should've tried sooner.

I fought the urge to reach out and touch. Aside from me holding his arm in the classroom to steady him—very awesome—we hadn't touched again. We'd taken separate showers. I was grateful for the spare bathroom down here in this full basement. Of course, I had to show Duncan how everything worked. He'd observed some things, but actual faucets had him flummoxed.

Oliver recounted his aunt and uncle offered him the room down here—to give him space—but that he hadn't wanted that distance. He'd made up an excuse and had taken the bedroom across from his aunt and uncle. I'd interpreted a bit of discomfort. As if Duncan and I would judge him.

We wouldn't. I'd been extremely close to my parents and my sister. Duncan had loved his wife. We understood needing to be close to someone.

"William, you need to sleep."

I jolted. "Were you not asleep?"

Duncan sighed. He'd been on his side, turned away from me. He rolled onto his back.

Oliver had kindly turned on a little lamp in the bathroom and only closed the door partway so we weren't in total darkness. Despite having been a ghost for all those years, I didn't like being unable to see anything. Duncan had gone along—whether to appease me or because he felt the same, I wasn't certain.

"You're thinking too much."

"Well…yeah." I lay on my side facing him, and I could make out his distinctive features in the low light. His beautiful skin. Cute nose. Sexy lips.

Sexy lips? That's what you're focusing on? Yep. Kissable lips. I'd only been lusting after him for a dozen years or so. Until recently, of course, I'd thought he was straight. Hearing he'd lusted after—or even loved—a fellow soldier had knocked me for a loop. *He* made me loopy. "I've never…" I drew breath. And strength. "When I came back to life, do you want to know what my first thought was?"

He turned to face me, his dark eyes glinting in the light. "William—"

I growled.

"Willie," he amended. "I never have any idea what you're thinking."

I wasn't certain that was true, but I soldiered on. "I thought I'd never see you again. And that made me sad.

I enjoy our conversations—infrequent that they are. I look forward to my time with you—even though I don't get the feeling you really like me."

He sighed. "You have no idea what I think or feel, Willie. I've always been a stoic man. I hold things close to my heart. I don't share." He snorted.

Which shocked me.

"I'm pretty certain your first thought was that you were naked." He took a deep breath. "Your sense of propriety dictated you would need clothes."

I considered. "Well, that came a close second. But, truly, you first. I was…sad. Until Hank came and found clothes for me—"

"Hank." He frowned. "And then he saw us again. Both rematerialized. This makes things interesting."

"He'll keep our secret."

"Oh, of that, I have no doubt." Duncan sighed. "We need rest, Willie. Tomorrow is going to be a long day. Oliver says he has an idea how to deal with our…dilemma. I have my doubts."

"From what I've seen, he's a good kid."

"He is." He remained quiet for a long time. "But he's only seventeen. Not yet an adult—in this time."

"No, for sure not." I hesitated. "I wouldn't have been either, in my time. Part of me feels fifty-two, and part of me still feels seventeen."

"You are both, my friend."

I bit my lower lip. "Do you really consider me a friend?"

He blinked. "Of course."

"Would you ever…could you ever…" I closed my eyes.

"Open your eyes, Willie."

I popped them open.

"Ask me, Willie."

"Will you…" I touched my lips.

His grin slowly appeared, but eventually, it became a full-on smile. "I'd be happy to."

"And would you, you know—"

"Another time…perhaps. We shall see."

"But we might, you know—"

"I know, Willie. Something tells me we'll have more than just one day."

"But that movie," I persisted. "Where the guy became a human and then the next day—"

"We aren't living in a movie, Willie. And he was an angel, not a ghost."

"You know which movie I'm talking about?"

"Mrs. Bletchley streams it at least once a month on her computer when no one is around."

"Yes." I sighed. "That's sad. I wish we could find her husband."

"Her husband might not have become a ghost. Can you imagine if every dead person was a ghost? That's a lot of people."

"I hadn't thought of it that way. So…we're the lucky ones?"

Duncan rolled on his side, facing me. "Yes, we're the lucky ones." He slowly feathered his hand through my hair. "This cut has to go." Then he grasped the back of my head and pulled me toward him.

I went willingly.

Our lips touched. Just feather-light.

The promise of something more.

When I tried to deepen it, though, he broke the kiss.

"Hey, we brushed our teeth and everything." I

pouted.

He grinned. "A novel experience for me. I always wondered what toothpaste tasted like. Now I know." His eyes…softened. "Turn on your side, Willie. I'll hold you tonight. Tomorrow we'll see what awaits."

I'd never been spooned before. Well, never had any guy touch me in *any* way before. I complied and tucked myself against his chest. His arm banded around me.

"I'll keep you safe. You never have to fear anything again."

Although not convinced he could keep all my demons at bay, I chose to believe him and soon slipped into rest.

That lasted until Oliver clomped down the stairs. "Oh, hey, I didn't mean—"

Duncan untangled himself first. "We were…comforting each other."

"Hey, no judgment here." He tossed clothes on the bed. "Duncan, you're about the same size as my uncle. Willie, I laundered your clothes from yesterday. We need to take you two shopping."

"We don't have any money." Duncan, pointing out the obvious.

"I think I have a solution for that." Oliver pointed to the clothes. "Hurry up." With that, he stomped back up the stairs.

Duncan cocked his head. "I thought carpeting made things less noisy."

"Teenage boys." Then I giggled. "I suppose I still am one."

"Hardly." He sorted through the clothes, eventually handing me the clean pile. "Now that I've figured out how to work the shower, I plan to take another one."

"Can we shower together?"

He gave me *that* look.

We showered separately.

Half an hour later, we poked our heads out of the basement.

Oliver waved us over to the kitchen table. "This is Duncan, and this is Willie."

His aunt rose. "You boys must be hungry. Waffles? Or I can do eggs. Poached? Fried? I'm Aunt Leslie, by the way. And this is Uncle Jeremiah."

"We're okay." I said those words because that was the polite response I'd been taught. Truthfully, the hastily constructed ham sandwiches from last night were, at least for me, a distant memory.

"No worries." She waved us off. "I have to cook for my boys anyway."

The man at the table cleared his throat.

She shot him an exasperated glare. "You cook every weekend, and usually, you're on the road by now. We're still an egalitarian partnership."

Oliver pointed to two empty chairs. "They don't want to be seen as traditional."

Duncan, as he sat, tilted his head.

"Like, women cook and clean…men work outside the home…" Oliver angled his chin to clearly encourage me to sit as well.

"But I can help," I offered. "I'm good at making waffles. Do you have a waffle iron?"

"Waffle iron?" Duncan stared at me. "Seriously?"

"Why don't you introduce me to your friends?" Oliver's uncle, Jeremiah, gazed between Duncan and me. "Something tells me you're going to have to be talking fast to explain why two strangers slept in our basement last night."

"I'm sorry—" Oliver tried.

His uncle held up his hand. "No recriminations. Just, next time wake me up. I wouldn't have said no." He muttered, "*Probably*."

He'd likely meant to do that under his breath, but I'd heard him. Or maybe he hadn't. I didn't know him well enough to guess. He had the same striking features as Duncan—elegant nose, full lips, high forehead, and short, curly hair. I didn't recognize him, so he hadn't gone to Pinedale. I didn't recognize Aunt Leslie, so she likely hadn't either.

"Right." Oliver fingered the sage-green cloth napkin before him. "So this is where you're going to have to suspend your disbelief."

Leslie snickered. "I teach second grade. I've heard it all."

Duncan and Jeremiah cleared their throats at the same time.

Oliver and I stilled while Leslie kept whisking batter.

"Start talking, young man. Your uncle moved his appointments today so he can help you out, whatever *help* means." She moved back to the kitchen.

Oliver drew a long breath and let it out slowly. "Uncle Jeremiah—"

The older man nodded.

"Well, I know this sounds absolutely goddamn crazy—"

I waited for a reprimand. None came. So either Oliver could get away with swearing or, more likely, his aunt and uncle realized how important this moment was.

"I need you to do something for me, and then we'll

never speak of this again." He pointed to Duncan. "This is your great-great-great-great-grandfather." He held himself still as that little grenade landed.

Jeremiah stared. Disbelief was clear, and when he started to speak, I expected a snicker. But he didn't. Instead he whispered, "Duncan Jeremiah?"

I was stunned he remembered the name. What, was he into this genealogy stuff? Maybe remembering was a game to him. That would be cool.

Oliver grabbed his phone and tapped a few times. "See this picture? That's part of his infantry. The Massachusetts 54th. He's second from the left." He handed his phone to his uncle. "Okay, it's really hard to see, and it's super fuzzy, but he says it's him, and I believe him." He glanced at Duncan.

Who nodded.

Jeremiah turned to Duncan. "You do look like him. Are you named after him? We'd be distant cousins…"

Duncan winced. "I am your distance relative." He glanced at Leslie. "My wife told me she had a new man in her life. I believe she spoke of my son." He cleared his throat. "She would not have wanted me to worry while I was in battle. In South Carolina. During the Civil War." He slowly nodded. "Juliette showed me the birth record of my son. That means…we are related."

"I don't…" Jeremiah rubbed his face. "You can't be *that* man."

"He can." I nearly wiggled off my seat. "We've been ghosts. For a long time. Well, him way longer than me, obviously."

Duncan gave me a look and then subtly shook his head.

"I don't…" Jeremiah opened and closed his mouth

179

several times but didn't finish his sentence.

"You all are ghosts?" Leslie eyed Duncan and me. "You don't look like ghosts."

"Oh, we, uh, rematerialized yesterday." I held out my hand.

She grabbed it, clearly thinking I meant for her to shake. She cocked her head as if not quite certain what to make of me.

"I couldn't do that yesterday."

"And your nose?"

Gingerly, I tapped it. "Yeah. I came back to life and walked into a wall. I used to be able to walk through them. Which is a super-freaky experience."

"I bet." She smiled. "Welcome back to the world of the living."

Unclear whether she truly believed me or not, but choosing to believe her kindness, I grinned. "Thank you."

"I'll have those waffles in a moment." She went back to the kitchen, which was separated from the dining room by a short wall. She kept coming out from behind it to talk to us, and I worried the waffles might burn. Truly, though, she appeared both competent and confident—two things I'd never been in real life. *But I'm going to do better*.

Jeremiah finally gave the photograph on Oliver's phone a quick glance. "I have a copy of this hanging in my home office."

"Right." Oliver snapped his fingers. "When I saw this last night, I was certain I'd seen it before. You showed it to me when you gave me the tour. You've got a picture of just about every generation, right?"

Duncan blinked. "You keep a photograph of me…"

Oliver leapt up. "Let me get it." He bounded up the stairs two at a time.

Jeremiah cleared his throat. "I have pictures of all of the first male descendants of every generation. Hard to believe, given how rare photographs are. We just…I guess we've always seen it as important. Starting with, I guess, your wife. I have an entire wall. My daddy, Jonathan, liked to remind me where we came from." He blinked. "The Jonathan he was named after would've been your stepson." He leaned forward. "How much do you know?"

I waited for Duncan to speak, but he remained silent. So I spoke up. Never had the sense God supposedly gave me. "Well, he'd left his regiment after the Battle of Boykin's Mill and was heading north when he was, uh, murdered. On what's now the grounds of Pinedale High. He's been a ghost since 1865."

Leslie spoke loudly from the kitchen. "I'm still listening, but these waffles are *not* burning while I'm running the kitchen."

"As opposed to me." Jeremiah's smile could only be termed rueful. "I have a habit of forgetting about them."

Oliver tromped down the stairs and joined us. "I didn't do much better when I had my turn." Clearly, he'd overheard Leslie's comment just before clomping down the stairs like an elephant. *Huh*. Duncan had never seen an elephant in person. *We should go to a zoo*.

Leslie laughed.

"This one." Oliver handed Duncan a framed photograph.

The man traced his fingers along the picture without actually touching the glass frame. "I remember this being taken."

Jeremiah held up his hand as if he needed a moment to take this all in or something.

Oliver sat. "I know this seems incredible. And, I mean, I get it if you don't believe me."

"You were a ghost?" Jeremiah's entire focus was on Duncan.

Duncan nodded.

I nodded too. Not that anyone seemed to be paying attention to me.

"And now you're not a ghost." Tentatively, he reached out a hand.

Duncan grasped it. "Corporal Duncan Jeremiah Galloway of the Massachusetts 54th Infantry."

They shook.

"I don't think I believed you. Until just now…" Jeremiah pointed to the photograph.

Leslie placed a plate of four massive waffles on the table. "One for each of you. I'll put on another batch. Something tells me you're hungry."

"What about you?" I wouldn't eat before she had.

She laughed. "Dear, I ate eggs and toast nearly an hour ago. Jeremiah's been stewing in his study, waiting for you to appear. Oliver said you needed rest."

"You're certain?" I pointed to the waffles.

She put a dish of butter and a bottle of my favorite genuine Vermont maple syrup on the table. "I'm sure." She eyed us all. "I think today's a big day. You're going to need sustenance." She met Oliver's gaze. "Do you need me to call in sick?"

Slowly, he shook his head. "I think we've got it covered."

She eyed Duncan. "You'll be here when I get back?"

He hesitated.

"They're not going anywhere until I get answers." Jeremiah slowly released Duncan's hand. "I suspect that's going to take all day."

By mutual agreement, we didn't speak again until we'd consumed our second waffles and Leslie headed off to school. Oliver and I put the plates in the dishwasher while Duncan watched with a grin and Jeremiah went upstairs to grab more photos.

We all sat around the table, avidly listening as he explained each Galloway in turn. Amazingly, each generation had a son who in turn had a son. Jeremiah was directly linked to Duncan. Truly, no DNA test was needed.

I'd learned about those things, hanging around the school. How guys needed to wear a rubber because if they knocked a girl up, they could administer a DNA test on the baby and that would identify the father. That had sounded far-fetched to me many years ago, but I'd heard of it happening and yeah, another reason to be glad I was in love with a man.

Wait.

My mind skidded to a halt as Jeremiah continued to speak—his words getting muddled in my mind as I grappled with the idea I might actually be in love with Duncan. We barely knew each other. Certainly not carnally. And yet my affection for him was stronger than anything I'd ever felt.

"So that's what I was thinking…" Oliver looked expectantly at Jeremiah.

Darn it all. I never had been able to pay attention for long. I was pretty certain, if I were in school today, that I'd be tested for ADD.

Jeremiah stilled. "That's a huge ask, Oliver."

"Not one I make lightly," Oliver countered in soft tones.

Slowly, I raised my hand. "Apologies. What did I miss?"

Duncan actually rolled his eyes at me. *Ha. Not always so chivalrous.*

"I'm asking Jeremiah to help arrange for you guys to get fake IDs."

"That's illegal." Jeremiah's jaw ticked. "I could lose my job."

"Well…" Oliver scratched his unshaven chin with a decent amount of stubble. "You could claim you were teaching us how to spot a fake one?"

"Or…" Jeremiah sighed. "I have an idea." He went on to explain that idea.

I didn't know much about taxes—except to be terrified of the IRS—but I sort of understood what he was willing to do for us. Nothing specifically illegal. But not truly aboveboard either. Still, if he happened to run a report and happened to leave the printout on his desk…

Twenty minutes later, we had a plan.

Chapter Nineteen

Peyton

I scrunched my nose in concentration. "So Willie and Duncan are just going to get social security cards from people who are likely dead? Asking for them because they *lost* them?" I eyed my friends, all crowded into my room.

Holden shrugged. "Jeremiah's got everything worked out. Then, somehow, they'll get photo IDs. Just to be safe, they're going to plan to live mostly off the grid."

"In Oregon." Oliver grinned. "Obviously, that was my idea."

Juliette gave him a charming smile. "Your uncle sounds amazing."

"He and Leslie want to get us all together next weekend. Big send-off for Willie and Duncan, if they can get all the documents together. Although Duncan could just be written off as Jeremiah's younger brother, Willie could attract attention. His mother and sister are still alive and living in Pinedale. As badly as Willie wants to see them, his mother's unwell, and him showing up might kill her." Oliver brushed a piece of lint off his jeans. "As soon as the IDs arrive, the guys are gone."

"Will we never see or hear from them again?" Juliette looked especially pained by this.

Of course she is. She knows Duncan personally. I'd tried to figure out if their relationship was more than just friendship, but I didn't see anything that would support that hypothesis. Neither had she mentioned Lucas once in all the times we'd been studying together. Of course, I hadn't found the courage to bring him up either. If she was dating the quarterback, though, I had yet to see any proof. Just lots of rumors.

"I found a refurbished laptop." Holden puffed out his chest a bit. "We got them signed up for free web mail accounts, and I'm going to teach them as much about computers as I can before they leave." He grinned. "Willie actually had a bit of experience. To hear him tell the story, the school computer he used was this big." He indicated a massive size, spanning almost the length of his arms.

I pursed my lips. "Really? That seems a bit of an exaggeration."

"Yet Willie doesn't seem prone to making things up." Oliver grinned. "Aunt Leslie cut his hair."

Juliette laughed. "Oh, I can't wait to see. Saturday night?"

"Yeah. Just come as you are. Leslie and Jeremiah are cooking up a storm, and I think they're planning to initiate Duncan and Willie in the kitchen as well. Off the grid doesn't necessarily mean they won't have electricity. Better they learn how to cook so they don't burn the place down." Oliver brushed at his jeans again before glancing at Holden.

"I learned early. What with taking care of Isabella." He yawned. "And I'm operating on a sleep deficit. I need to get going."

He was still tired? Seeing as we were now at

Thursday, I wasn't certain why. We'd just had practice and had congregated back at my place. Juliette and I had done some studying of derivatives so she'd pass her test.

"I'll walk you out." Oliver rose as well.

"I know the way out." Holden grinned.

"Right. I just meant…" Oliver snapped his mouth shut.

"What he means is that he was leaving as well." Juliette made a sweeping motion, likely meaning the two guys should head out.

"Of course." Oliver snagged his backpack. "Let's leave the ladies alone, Holden."

Holden glanced at me, snorted, then sobered as he seemed to notice Juliette's rather unimpressed expression. "I just meant—"

Oliver snagged his elbow. "Before you talk yourself into even more trouble." He did a little bow. "You're both wonderful. I…" He nodded. "I think we did a good thing." He glanced at Holden. "So I guess I should thank you."

My best friend puffed out his chest. "You just call anytime."

Oliver had recounted his discussion with Principal Kouriki. We'd agreed he had enormous balls to make the decision to come forward. But if that meant other kids didn't get bullied, then the decision would be worth it. Tonight, before practice, Coach Pinker had sat the entire football team down and read them the riot act. If anyone was found to be bullying anyone, they were off the squad permanently as well as facing suspension. Apparently, all the teams would be getting the same message. Word was getting around—no bullying.

In no way did I believe this would put an end to it,

but I could see Oliver getting through the rest of his senior year unscathed. Gary wasn't going to risk his scholarship. Dominic was only in eleventh grade, so he risked even more. And basketball wasn't in full swing, so Larry faced more consequences about court time if he screwed around. No, for this year at least, we'd be left in peace.

Holden waved as Oliver herded him out. Seeing as they knew the way, I didn't bother to escort them to the door. My parents were in the family room watching television, so one of them might get up to lock the door.

Probably not. Pinedale was a pretty safe town.

"Okay, are you ready to try again?" I pointed to my calculus textbook. I sat at my desk with Juliette next to me. She was plopped on a kitchen chair Oliver had brought in for her while he and Holden had rested on my bed. Well, he'd perched. Holden had sprawled.

Juliette pulled even closer. "Yes. Show me how this works again?"

I tapped my pencil on the textbook. "So you take…"

She took my hand in hers.

I froze. "What?"

"Is this okay?" She met my gaze with beguiling dark-brown eyes. Her hair cascaded around her face, and she was heart-stoppingly beautiful. Yet what I loved most about her was how she was on the inside. Just a genuinely good person.

I smiled. "Of course."

She returned my smile. "Cool. Now, you were saying…"

Chapter Twenty

Holden

As I sat at Oliver's dining room table, I had my hand resting on his shoulder.

We'd lost our division's championship game.

No state finals for us.

Jeremiah had live streamed the game so Duncan and Willie could watch here at the house, then he and Leslie had come home after the game.

The band, cheer squad, and team had hung around a little longer. To commiserate. The other team outmatched us at every turn.

Except field-goal kicking. Oliver nailed every kick he got.

Three turnovers, however, destroyed any potential momentum on our side. We didn't get routed, but we did get our asses handed to us.

Now, as Duncan, Willie, Oliver, and I ate pizza, I took a moment to admire the former ghosts. They touched constantly. Gave each other special smiles. Completed each other's sentences. In other words—they looked like a couple.

Getting them organized was taking longer than expected, but Leslie and Jeremiah had no problems with their uninvited guests. Jeremiah spent hours on end sharing family stories with his four-times grandfather.

He'd always been the keeper of history in his family, and slowly, he was also sharing that information with Oliver.

I got the feeling that if Jeremiah and Leslie didn't wind up having children, or if their children weren't interested in family lore, Jeremiah would be thrilled for Oliver to take that role.

Oliver, for his part, seemed keen.

One night, we'd snuck back into school with Duncan and Willie. They couldn't see or talk to the other ghosts. They'd talked to each other, though. Discussed how they'd rematerialized. What life was like outside of school grounds. How they hoped other ghosts would follow their examples, if they wished, and find their own way back. Maybe next semester a ghost might break through. Willie had made it clear they could come to see me and I'd take care of them. That seemed a little much, but I'd do just about anything to support my new friends, and if that meant shepherding their friends, I'd do it.

None of the six of us had seen another ghost. Knowing they were watching, and some of them even speaking to each other, felt oddly creepy and yet weirdly reassuring.

Also, Duncan and Willie had tried talking to Hank. He'd clammed up, claiming he had no idea how the ghost thing worked.

None of us believed him.

Willie snapped his fingers in front of my face.

I scowled.

He grinned. "I said Duncan and I are headed downstairs."

To the bed they shared together every night. Part of me was intensely curious about what they got up to down there, and the rest of me knew it was none of my goddamned business.

"When do you leave?"

Duncan cleared his throat. "Jeremiah requested we stay past Christmas. Just another couple of weeks."

"He's located a farm that is looking for employees. Hazelnut as well as greenhouses year-round. A big operation needing plenty of help." Willie grinned. "Some distant relative of one of Jeremiah's friends who died. Jeremiah reached out, and they got to talking, and apparently, the family scattered after reconstruction, and some headed west. Made it all up and down the west coast from Los Angeles to Spokane. This branch settled near Canby, Oregon."

"Wow." My mind whirled. "So Jeremiah calls up to discuss a long-dead relative, and you two get a job?"

Duncan nodded. "Providential."

"Horseshoe-up-your-ass lucky, I say."

"And so you just did." Oliver gave me a look I couldn't decipher.

"We're off." Duncan rose, holding his hand out.

Willie took it, rising as well.

They nodded at us and headed downstairs.

Oliver collected the empty pizza boxes. "I need to throw these in the garbage, or they'll stink up the house."

I sniffed experimentally. "Nothing wrong with a good cheese-and-tomato smell."

He chuckled. "True." Still, he rose.

I collected the empty glasses and carried them to the kitchen, then followed him to the garage. "I guess I should go home."

Oliver tossed the boxes, then shrugged. "It's up to you. Is your mother working tonight? Is Isabella alone?"

"Isabella turned thirteen last week and has declared

she's able to stay alone from now on."

"Is that the law?"

I grinned. "Isabella's law." I shrugged. "Technically, the law said she could when she turned eight."

Oliver's jaw dropped. "Okay, back home the age was at least ten. I wasn't fit to be left alone at ten, let alone eight."

"Different states. Mom's done her best, but there've been a few times over the years. If I go away for school next year, Isabella's going to be alone all the time. She'll be in high school, though, so that'll be okay." Mom and Isabella had come to the game. They'd both given me consolation hugs, and Mom had told me to have fun tonight but to be careful. Her mantra for her kids.

"What school?" Oliver gestured for me to go back into the house.

"I applied to the Columbia School of Journalism, journalism at Temple University, and UNC Hussman School of Journalism and Media." I rattled these off without thought. "But I doubt I can afford New York City. Philly's pretty steep too. In-state tuition if I go to Chapel Hill."

Oliver shepherded me into the family room.

I dropped onto the oversized leather sectional.

He sat right beside me instead of at the other end.

Great. Torture me all over again. First watching him in his uniform. Then enjoying pizza with him. Now some quality alone time—which we almost never got. "Which school are you thinking? Hell, I don't even know what you plan to major in."

He waved me off. Then wiggled his butt a bit before sighing. "So there was an incident yesterday."

I swiveled my head to look at him.

He didn't meet my gaze. "Dwayne…he made a comment about me hanging out with the *queers*." He said the word with air quotes.

I had a quick retort, but something had me holding my tongue. This was his story to tell.

"But Lucas asked what was wrong that." He frowned, as if working out something in his mind.

I waited.

He closed one eye, as if contemplating his next words. "And Dwayne said people would start talking. And Lucas told him to fuck off. That we were past living in the 1950s. That any kind of bigotry was wrong." He rubbed his forehead. "The other guys laughed. Some at me, I think. I mean, some guys agree with Dwayne. But more were laughing at him. Not really in a bad way, but in a way they were glad someone finally put him in his place."

"And with Lucas being the star quarterback and the captain of the team…"

"Yeah. His words meant something. And a few weeks ago, someone made a comment about Peyton and Juliette. Lucas put him in his place. Said he was thrilled the two were together."

I grinned. "They do make a cute couple. I thought Lucas was with Juliette… Was he hurt?"

"They were never together. I think…well, Lucas is *very* open-minded, if you know what I mean." Oliver settled back on the couch.

"I don't know what you mean."

"Well, he's been hanging around Lou's Diner a lot."

"Oliver, all the cool kids hang out there." Which reminded me that I hadn't been for a while. We'd need to go so I could keep up my cool persona. *Who are you kidding? Oh, wait…no one!* "Too bad we can't take Duncan and Willie."

He cocked his head. "We could sneak them in on a quiet night. Morgan wouldn't recognize Willie, of course. Just don't let Martha get a good look at him."

"With that haircut he really looks different." I considered. "Something to ask. But you got me off track."

"Holden, you did that all by yourself." He grinned. "What I'm trying to say is Lucas's been spending an awful lot of time at the diner."

"And?" Fatigue was beginning to set in.

"I think he and Morgan are hanging out more."

I grinned. "That's nice. Morgan can use more friends. More people believing in them."

"Yeah." Oliver flicked a piece of lint off his jeans. I could never figure out how his jeans attracted so much lint. "So Willie made a comment…"

"Oh dear."

"Yeah." He chuckled. "He said his fantasy could never have come true because no one who looked like Frank—that douchebag he fancied himself in love with—played football and was gay."

"He was saying football players couldn't be gay?"

"He was saying he didn't know any."

"Did you tell him about that college player who came out?"

"No. I didn't figure that would have an impact on him. But I did say I knew one personally."

That got my attention. "One of the guys on the squad? Okay, I'm intensely curious, and if I wasn't so exhausted, I would try to guess."

He shifted but didn't meet my gaze. "I said me."

Did he just… Yeah, he did. Christ, say something. "You're gay?"

"Yep. Always have been. I didn't come out to my parents, but my grandmother knows. I might've casually told Leslie and Jeremiah after I brought our former ghosts home. Just casual like."

"And how'd they take it?"

"Casual like."

That sounded exactly like what Leslie and Jeremiah would do. Just good, honest folk. Well, aside from helping with false identities. Jeremiah seemed to have gotten over his scruples with his part in this entire scheme. Setting right a long-ago wrong.

"Okay." I frowned. "So is there anyone in our group who isn't gay?"

Oliver remained silent.

"I guess us gays sort of stick together then, right?"

"Yep."

"And you don't mind me waiting for you after practice?" I'd tried to be subtle…but everyone knew subtlety was so *not* my strength.

"Of course I don't mind. Why would I?"

"If you hang around me too much, people will start to talk." I'd tried to be discreet for this exact reason. He didn't need the hassle.

"What do you think they'll say?"

"Like you're my boyfriend. Because I'm gay, you know." I tried for a moment of levity.

"Well, so am I."

"So you, uh, don't mind if people think…"

"I care what *you* think."

"What do you mean?" My head was spinning as if

195

I'd drunk a couple of shots, even though I hadn't.

Oliver finally turned to face me. He angled his body so he was just an inch away from me. "Holden, do you want me to be your boyfriend?"

"Well, *duh*. Wasn't I there, on the first day of school, defending your honor? I've liked you from the start. Of course I'd love to be your boyfriend."

"I seem to recall Peyton threatening to wield a clarinet—"

"Oh, shuddup. I was right there." I gazed into his fathomless blue eyes. "Are you serious?"

He grinned. "I liked you too. Have this entire time. I just didn't know how to tell you."

"Well, maybe like saying, 'Holden, I like you'?"

"Holden, I like you."

"Great. Because I like you too."

He inched toward me.

I leaned in.

Our lips brushed.

Epilogue

Duncan
Six Years Later

I entered the cabin I shared with my husband and stomped my boots.

"Hey." He waved from the kitchen. "Did you get that drainage issue fixed?"

"Yes." I removed my raincoat. "How is it that your computer swears Boston gets more rain than us?"

"Rain totals vary from year to year and also our specific location." He waved me off as he stirred something delicious in the pot. "You're always carrying on about Boston." He frowned. "Do you want to go there? For a visit? Or to live? It would be very—"

Gently, I eased my arm around his waist and pressed my cold cheek to the back of his neck.

He squealed. Which was distinctive from his squeaking. Which also amused me.

He tried to bat me away. "I'm cooking pasta sauce. Go take a shower and warm up."

I headed over to the gas fireplace. We didn't use it often, but on cold, wet nights like tonight, we splurged. "You knew I'd come home like this."

He laughed. "Yes. And I get cow duty in the morning, so I'm not staying up late."

"I think I got the better deal." I held my hands out to

the flame, letting the warmth invade my bones. So many nights, during the war, I'd lain awake at night. Cold. Alone.

I glanced over at my adorable *hubby*. *I'll never be alone again.* Well, so long as we stayed healthy. We'd yet to confide in a doctor that we'd been ghosts for extended periods of time. I'd expected more…issues. Aside from the occasional ache deep in my bones on damp days, I encountered no ill effects from my death. That I could tell. Willie said much the same.

"Oh, I forgot to tell you something." He removed the pot from the burner and got out two plates. "You're hungry now?"

"Starving. That ditch took longer to clear. John helped, though, and we got it done." John was another farmhand. The farm owners—Liliana and Marvin—were aging gracefully. And happily letting us younger folk do the heavy lifting.

We loved our generous employers. We were happy to do the heavy lifting.

"Parmesan?" Willie headed to the fridge after placing two heaping plates of spaghetti on the table.

I plopped onto my kitchen chair. "I love you."

He laughed as he put a glass of milk before me and a soda for himself. He went back to the fridge and returned with parmesan. Some people kept it in the cupboard, but we always had it in the fridge to preserve its freshness. Truthfully, I loved my fridge. Of all the modern wonders, that was near the top. "Oh, you said you had something to tell me."

Willie sat in his chair. He took a sip of his soda with ice.

I teased him about cavities.

He said he'd missed soda most while a ghost. Said it tongue in cheek. What he'd really missed was his family.

Aunt Leslie had found an excuse to approach Willie's sister. They'd struck up a friendship. Through Leslie, we got periodic updates about Willie's sister and mother. His mother wasn't well. As much as Willie wanted to go back, he never would.

The photos Leslie sent had to be enough.

"Yes." Willie swallowed a mouthful of pasta. "So good."

Tomato sauce in a jar. Another wonder.

"I got an email from Holden."

"Oh?"

Although Willie and I were both competent on the computer, his skills exceeded mine. And he typed far faster than I ever could.

"Rolls!" He leapt from the table.

"I could've gotten those." He'd only been home about an hour before me after a long day.

"They're not fresh baked." He donned an oven mitt and pulled a plate from the oven. He flipped the heat off, then came to me and used a mitt to cover his hand so he could drop a roll on my plate. "I don't need to tell you they're hot."

I chuckled. "No, you do not." I eyed the butter. *How long do I have to wait?* As much as I loved pasta, I loved rolls even more. The scent reminded me of the bread Mama had baked for the White folks, that we slaves never got so much as a bite of, except the stale crumbs thrown out. I liked thinking Mama was watching me eat warm fresh white bread now, as much as I wanted, in my own safe home.

During our time of waiting while Jeremiah organized everything for us, Holden and Oliver had run many searches. Even with what I'd provided from memory, they hadn't located a trace of either my mother or my three younger siblings. Lost to history, apparently. The south had been chaotic after the war, and many records had been destroyed. I could only hope they survived. They might've taken another name, of course. As I had—taking the name of a Black freedman I respected greatly. I'd needed to hide my identity near the beginning of the war. And since my original surname had been that of my master, I'd chosen to keep Galloway. I'd married my sweetheart, thereby making her my wife and giving her my new name. Then she'd birthed a child whose existence she kept from me. My son. A Galloway.

That name now tied me to a long list of distinguished men—including Jeremiah.

Willie plopped back into his seat. "Holden and Oliver want to come and visit." He buttered his roll.

I did the same. "When?"

"After Christmas." He grinned. "I think they're wanting to make the move out here. Even though Oliver's grandmother's gone, he still feels an affinity to Oregon. He really loves Portland."

"What about Pinedale?" Holden's mother still lived there, although his sister now attended Brown University in Rhode Island on a scholarship. Destined for greatness, Isabella was.

Willie shrugged. "They both love Pinedale, but after New York City…"

Holden had been accepted to his beloved Columbia School of Journalism, and Oliver had snuck in a last-minute application to their architecture school. They'd complained plenty about the years spent in a tiny walkup apartment with invincible roaches, but they'd been happy.

"Do they have prospects?"

Not that they needed them. The insurance settlement from Oliver's parents' death had paid for their housing and his schooling. Holden had secured scholarships and worked part time to help pay the bills. We'd received missive after missive of their time in the *Big Apple*.

Occasionally, we'd discuss visiting, but Willie and I were homebodies. And why attract attention to ourselves? At least we were aging at what appeared to be a normal rate. Hopefully, that meant we'd have a good life expectancy as well.

After swallowing a delicious mouthful of roll, I moaned.

"Keep that up, and we're going to wind up in bed."

"I thought we were heading there anyway." I winked.

He blushed. Six years on and just the mere hint of sex made him blush. For a guy who'd been naked for thirty-five years, he was still a bit of a prude.

My prude.

And I loved him. More every day.

"What about Leslie and Jeremiah?"

"Don't forget Jonathan and Carly." Their twins. Jonathan for the son Duncan's wife bore after she remarried. A man who'd also distinguished himself, although had not had children. Carly for Oliver's mother, Caroline. The four-year-old twins were, to hear Leslie complain, little menaces.

Jeremiah sent pictures nearly every day of the two beautiful children they'd had after several treatments of

IVF. Another modern miracle wonder.

Willie waved his fork. "Right, I didn't get to the best part. Jeremiah applied for a job at the Portland field office."

"I thought he wanted to get back to Washington. Isn't that where the important jobs are?"

"Uh, yeah." He twirled his spaghetti onto his fork. "According to Holden, on their last visit to Pinedale, Jeremiah admitted he was happy with fieldwork and that family was more important than any *DC job*. Holden says they're looking at Beaverton. Or even Alberta."

My fork clattered to the plate. "That's close to us."

He grinned. "Jeremiah asked me to keep it quiet until Holden and Oliver made their decision. If the boys wanted to go back to Pinedale, I think Leslie and Jeremiah would've stayed. But seeing as the boys want to move west—"

"*Boys?*" I chuckled. "They're your age, my dear."

That grin got wider. "Or I'm decades older."

I snagged his hand and brought it to my lips. "You'll always be young to me."

He scowled. "I'd like to be seen as an equal."

I scowled. "Of course you are."

"Gotcha."

After a moment, I smiled. "Yes, you did." I eyed my pasta, trying to determine if I had enough room to eat all of it and still have space for the vanilla ice cream I adored.

Willie loved chocolate.

"Oh, speaking of hearing, how are Juliette and Peyton doing?"

He squinted his left eye. Something he did when he was thinking really hard. "I thought I told you about their last email."

"Remind me."

"Peyton is happily teaching music, secure in her mother's satisfaction that Lily's working for NASA." Having an engineer for an older sister lessened the pressure on Peyton to follow into some profession that required physics and, potentially, biology. Calculus didn't help her with teaching little kids how to play the recorder, but she loved her life.

"Okay, so no changes there."

"Nope." He waved his fork. "But I know I told you Juliette got into the PhD program for psychology at Harvard."

I blinked. "We really need to work on your sharing skills."

"I told you." He offered up the protest even as he winked. "Or was that the day you came home and dragged me—"

"Don't blame my…desire to have you…on your inability to remember to tell me important things."

He shrugged. "Well, Juliette's parents wanted her to study medicine at Harvard. Instead, she's doing experimental psychopathology."

I might've blinked again. "Okay, well, we need to look into the program so I can sound vaguely intelligent when she calls." A thought occurred. "Is Peyton with her in Cambridge?"

"Yes, teaching at a public school. They've got a little apartment and are thrilled." He pointed. "I'm sure I told you this. I think your memory's failing you."

"No." I stuck my chin in the air. I was pretty certain I would've remembered all this great news. Circling back, I smiled. "You think Holden and Oliver will stay?"

"Oliver's applied for a master's degree at U of O. He'd be in Eugene, but I'm sure Jeremiah will give them the money to buy a car."

"What's Holden going to do in Eugene?"

Willie bit his lip. "I forgot—"

I gesticulated wildly. "Seriously?"

"He landed a job with the *Associated Press*. After doing two years with *The Brooklyn Eagle*, he applied."

"Just like that."

"Just like that." He offered a sly smile. "There's an AP bureau in Portland."

"But Oliver's studying in Eugene."

"Just his coursework. Then he can transfer to Portland. They'll only be apart for short times. Remember how I said Jeremiah might buy them a car?"

My eyes narrowed. "All this? From one email?"

He bit his lower lip again. "Okay, this has been in the works for months, but I didn't want you to get your hopes up. When we moved out here, we knew it'd be really tough not to see your family from back east."

"And now you're saying…"

"If everything goes as planned, they should be here in early summer. In time for the twins to get registered in school. In time for Oliver to get settled before he begins his graduate studies. In time for Jeremiah, Holden, and Leslie to start their new jobs."

"Leslie?"

"Portland's school board is hiring. She'll easily get something."

"That simple?"

"Yep. That simple."

This would cut our final direct tie to Pinedale. We'd tried to keep track, through Leslie and Jeremiah, but if any other ghosts had escaped, word had not filtered back to us. We hoped, if such an occurrence happened, they would be just as good at hiding. I was glad, after walking the school for so many years and hearing the language and slang as it changed, that I could speak to others and not sound too old-fashioned.

I grasped Willie's hand. "Okay. I want to call them."

"I thought you might. Then ice cream and then bed." He rose. "I'll do the dishes while you make the calls."

"No." I rose as well. "The dishes can wait. Speakerphone is a wonderful thing. I want to hear how you talk yourself out of keeping all this from me for so long."

He pinkened. "Then bed?"

"Count on it." I pulled him into my arms.

He tipped his head back. "The day I rematerialized and left the school with Holden was the worst of my life because I thought I'd never see you again."

I cocked my head.

"Uh." He appeared to contemplate. "Did you rematerialize before or after midnight? Because if you came back before midnight, then it would've been the best day ever, and if the miracle happened after midnight, then *that* would've been the best day ever."

I blinked. "I love you."

He laughed. "Me too."

Our lips met.

"Forever." I whispered the word with reverence.

"Forever." He affirmed my word, then kissed me again.

We didn't get to that phone call for a while longer.

A word about the author…

USA Today bestselling author Gabbi Grey lives in beautiful British Columbia where her fur baby chin-poo keeps her safe from the nasty neighborhood squirrels. Working for the government by day, she spends her early mornings writing contemporary, gay, sweet, and dark erotic BDSM romances. While she firmly believes in happy endings, she also believes in making her characters suffer before finding their true love. She also writes M/F romances as Gabbi Black and Gabbi Powell.

~*~

Visit Gabbi Grey online at:
www.gabbigrey.com

Thank you for purchasing
this publication of The Wild Rose Press, Inc.

For questions or more information
contact us at
info@thewildrosepress.com.

The Wild Rose Press, Inc.
www.thewildrosepress.com

www.ingramcontent.com/pod-product-compliance
Lightning Source LLC
Chambersburg PA
CBHW051650260626
47170CB00004B/1434